Damiana's Reprieve

Damiana's Reprieve

Novella for two voices

Martha Bátiz

translated by
Gustavo Escobedo

EXILE
e d i t i o n s

Publishers of Singular
Fiction, Poetry, Nonfiction, Translation, Drama and Graphic Books

Library and Archives Canada Cataloguing in Publication

Bátiz, Martha
[Boca de lobo. English]
Damiana's reprieve : novella for two voices / Martha Bátiz ;
translated by Gustavo Escobedo.

Translation of: Boca de lobo.
English translation previously published in 2009 under title: The wolf's mouth.
Issued in print and electronic formats.
ISBN 978-1-55096-798-2 (softcover).--ISBN 978-1-55096-799-9 (EPUB).
--ISBN 978-1-55096-800-2 (Kindle).--ISBN 978-1-55096-801-9 (PDF).

I. Escobedo, Gustavo, 1968-, translator II. Title. III. Title: Boca de lobo. English.

PS8553.A8295B6213 2018   C863'.7   C2018-904736-4
                                                                   C2018-904737-2

Copyright © Martha Bátiz, 2018
Text and cover design by Michael Callaghan
Cover photo Shutterstock / back cover Igor Bulgarin
Typeset in Birka at Moons of Jupiter Studios

Published by Exile Editions Limited – www.ExileEditions.com
144483 Southgate Road 14 – GD, Holstein, Ontario, N0G 2A0
Printed and bound in Canada by Marquis

We gratefully acknowledge the Canada Council for the Arts,
the Government of Canada, the Ontario Arts Council,
and the Ontario Media Development Corporation
for their support toward our publishing activities.

Canadian sales representation:
The Canadian Manda Group, 664 Annette Street,
Toronto ON M6S 2C8 www.mandagroup.com 416 516 0911

North American and international distribution, and U.S. sales:
Independent Publishers Group, 814 North Franklin Street,
Chicago IL 60610 www.ipgbook.com toll free: 1 800 888 4741

For Edgar, Ivana, Natalia, and Marco,
the loves of my life.

DRAMATIS PERSONAE

The Guerra Family

DAMIANA GUERRA . . . . *opera singer*

TAMARA GUERRA . . . . *her sister*

EDUARDO ("LALITO") GUERRA . . . . *her brother*

EUSEBIO GUERRA . . . . *her father*

The Marriage of Figaro ~ Cast

DAMIANA GUERRA . . . . *Susanna (Figaro's bride)*

DIMITRI . . . . *Figaro*

ELENA . . . . *Cherubino*

MICHAELA . . . . *Countess Rosina*

GUIDO . . . . *orchestra conductor*

JUAN JOSÉ . . . . *stage director*

MARISITA . . . . *choir director, a retired soprano*

FAUSTINA . . . . *Damiana's assistant/helper*

RODRIGO . . . . *a violinist*

MARILÚ . . . . *Elena's niece*

~ Other Beaumarchais/Mozart characters that appear in this story: the COUNT ALMAVIVA (*a Spanish nobleman*), BARTOLO (*the Countess' one-time guardian*), MARCEL-LINA (*Bartolo's housekeeper*), BARBARINA (*the gardener's daughter*).

~ Additional characters: *musicians, theatre technicians, a* (bald) *music critic, bureaucrats, a doctor.*

The action begins in the Palace of Fine Arts (Palacio de Bellas Artes or "Bellas Artes"), the main Opera House in Mexico City, minutes prior to the opening night of Mozart's *The Marriage of Figaro*. The story takes place over the course of five days, starting on a Tuesday evening and ending on Saturday night.

Brief Summary of
Mozart's *The Marriage of Figaro*
(*Le nozze di Figaro*)

The action is divided into four acts. It takes place in a single day at the Almaviva country residence in Spain (close to Seville), in the 17th century. Figaro and Susanna, personal servants to Count Almaviva and his wife, respectively, are about to get married. Susanna knows that the Count wants to seduce her and warns Figaro about it. Bartolo and Marcellina try to stop the wedding. They have an IOU of Figaro's: it promises his marriage to old Marcellina if his debt goes unpaid. Bartolo supports Marcellina's demand because he is still angry at Figaro for having helped the Count steal Rosina (now his wife, the Countess) from him. For Bartolo, seeing Figaro married to Marcellina – instead of Susanna – is the perfect revenge. Susanna and Marcellina have a confrontation, but Susanna does not know about the IOU. Cherubino, the hormone-raging teenage page, seeks Susanna's help to hide him from the Count. He has been found in a compromising situation with young Barbarina, and now the Count says he must leave. The problem is that Cherubino falls immediately in love with every woman he sees, or so he thinks, and he gets into constant trouble for it. The Count starts pursuing Susanna more aggressively, thinking he can get away with it. The Countess is heartbroken because her husband does not pay attention to her anymore, and she misses him terribly. Susanna knows this. She and Figaro become the Countess' accomplices in teaching the Count a lesson that will bring him back to his wife. Meanwhile, Cherubino pretends to go away as a soldier as the Count has requested, but instead stays in the house courting Susanna, the Countess, Barbarina and whoever else is close to him – all the while hiding from the Count (which accounts for some of the funniest scenes in the opera). At the same time, Figaro has to find a way to not marry Marcellina. Susanna finds out about the debt and is ready to pay it so he's free to marry her. Before she can do so, Figaro argues that he needs parental consent in order to marry Marcellina. However, since he is a foundling, getting parental consent is impossible. When he shows his birthmark to Bartolo and Marcellina, it is discovered that Figaro is, in fact, their son. Marcellina and Figaro embrace lovingly at the very moment Susanna enters the scene ready to pay her groom's debt. She thinks he's betraying her and slaps him, but once she finds out the truth, everyone is joyous. There will be a double wedding now: Figaro/Susanna and Bartolo/Marcellina. Figaro and Susanna, with the Countess' help, continue with their plans to teach the Count a lesson so he will remain faithful to his wife. After much confusion, there is a happy ending for them all.

❧ 1 ❧

There are eight lightbulbs framing the mirror, but one does not work. It blinks, distracting me. The bulbs are covered in a thin layer of dust that I've been meaning to clean since the beginning of rehearsals, but I keep forgetting.

"Your attention, please. First curtain call."

The sound of the musicians tuning their instruments can be heard in the background.

The announcement continued: "Members of the orchestra, please proceed to the pit."

Even though I should be used to these calls, I'm always startled. I never notice how late it is. Elena, Dimitri, and some musicians had left not long ago, but none of them seemed in a rush. *I have been vocalizing since I shut the door. Each note has grown exact, and vibrates in harmony. But even this certainty has not helped with my trembling knees. The palms of my hands are sweaty, and I feel as though a rat, on the run, is churning in my entrails.* Perhaps this would have been better said with less frankness. It could be misinterpreted. But I decided not to cross it out. Instead, I added: *It is strange to articulate this, to put it in writing.* No one had ever asked me to respond to a written interview before an opening night – minutes before an opening night. I only accepted because it was for Elena's favourite niece. Also because I could respond at my own pace. And because I wanted to put words to this fear. Evidently, it had not been a good idea. *The pen is slipping from my grasp. Forgive me, Marilú: I cannot concentrate.*

That was the last thing I wrote that afternoon in the dressing room. I had, in fact, already answered all the questions that required something more structured, standard, and even optimistic.

I forced myself to appear strong as I walked across the stage and opened the velvet curtain to peer at the empty hall. Rising before my eyes were three storeys of balconies and seating so immense and red that it seemed I was standing before the mouth of a beast – a beast ready to devour me. *What am I doing here?* A trembling chin announced tears, but I tightened my fists and did not allow myself to falter. No matter what, I was not going to break down in front of Rodrigo. I knew that he was watching me from behind a wall in the set. I wouldn't allow myself to ruin my makeup minutes before the performance. The audience was about to enter.

It was then that Dimitri, Elena, and the others joined me to admire that silent space that would soon be teeming with life. They were all cheerful as they walked me back to my dressing room. Rodrigo gave me a look that I failed to avoid in time. He was almost unrecognizable. Insignificant? Yes, maybe so. Shrunken, without a doubt. It made me sad but I feigned indifference. I entered the dressing room and I shut the door behind me. On it, written on a piece of paper that was crudely affixed with Scotch tape, my name in capitals: DAMIANA GUERRA. When I saw it for the first time I had the feeling that it was someone else's name, not mine, but I didn't really care. *It is a strange feeling, you know? Years waiting and anticipating success, and when it arrives at last, everything is once again a new beginning.*

This was the first time I didn't have to share a dressing room. I hadn't told anyone that the character of Susanna was the first to allow me this privilege. Not even when I played Adina in Donizetti's *The Elixir of Love* was I granted such privacy. This protagonist's solitude had been a relief since my arrival. I had arranged my things just the way I like them. I was able to unpack down to the last of the jars I carry in my vanity case and lay them out on the counter according to their size and contents (twelve on the counter to balance out the eight lightbulbs and four in the bathroom – when I get nervous I start counting everything). I turned on the humidifier so that the dry polluted air would not hurt my throat; I organized my wardrobe in the requisite order, and then spent a long while reading and considering the questions that Marilú had given me. She was so excited about my participation in her school project that she even gave me the notebook to write in . . .

Everything had been fine until the memories brewing in the back of my mind started to hurt, so I decided to put the questionnaire aside and attend to my makeup. *This is part of the magic: to exaggerate the features, to lend one's skin to a character, to give the character a face.* Hiding behind someone else's face makes everything easier. At least that is what I thought – until Tamara came along.

Once in character, I brought out my thermos and drank tea with honey in silence, enjoying each sip, and observing the photograph with care. Although I always bring it with me, I rarely tuck it into the edge of the mirror in the dressing rooms of the theatres where I sing. Pictures in dressing rooms bring back bad memories. Besides, whenever people see the the pictures, they ask questions, and I feel uncomfortable, and so it had been a long time since I had sat down to look at this one. The years had eaten into its colours. It was damaged. At times, I had thought I should get a picture frame to protect it, but I'd only remembered this when I found it once again in the side pocket of my vanity case. That evening, I was taken aback at how faded the image was. The colours in the picture had once been as brilliant on paper as they were in my memory: Tamara's bright red bell-bottomed trousers, Father's yellow shirt, Mother in such white that it hurt to look, Eduardo dressed up as a policeman, and me in that dress that I wore until it fit me no longer. Those were our faces, our clothes, but it wasn't us. I had never before or after seen Father smile with such contentment. It was never said out loud, but that had been the last happy moment of our childhood. Tamara, Eduardo, and I soon lost that light, that shine very deep in the eyes that can be seen in the photo. Mother was radiant, but I cannot remember her laughter as she plucked a flower with her toes and gave it to Father. She liked going barefoot and could grasp any light object with her feet and lift it anywhere. Father enjoyed this. As if by instinct, I tried to move my toes independently inside Susanna's boots. I knew that I wouldn't be able to do so.

Faustina was supposed to take care of arranging my things because I don't trust the women in charge of wardrobe. Wanting to feel ownership of the dressing room, however, I had asked her to leave me alone as soon as we entered the theatre. I wished to dress my character slowly – "*To be calm,*" I told her. But we had arrived so early that I was ready much too soon, and I regretted it. I wanted to stop thinking about the very personal questions in Marilú's school interview. Adolescents are like that – curious – and she had always been curious, more so than any child I had ever met. I no longer wanted to look at the photograph that I had stuck on the mirror by the third lightbulb. That is why I had decided to go for a stroll and have a look through the curtain. The empty seats look so different during rehearsals. It is as if they don't really exist, especially if one knows the space already, but afterwards . . . In truth, I was searching for someone to stop me from running away – to give me courage. Fortunately, seeing Dimitri and Elena made me feel safe.

When the musicians began to tune their instruments, and the horns, the strings, the woodwinds, the musical scales, and the voices of the other singers combined with mine through the speakers and the walls (bare and of a desolate and worn-out white – why are dressing rooms so ugly?), I wanted to believe that even if it was only my face in all the mirrors I looked into, that even in spite of everything, I was happy. It was futile. *I love to sing, but I hate everything before I come out on stage.* I definitely wrote such sentiments down in some part of that notebook. Besides, I found it hard to concentrate with the noise of the cars choking the main street outside. My dressing room's window in Mexico City's Palace of Fine Arts – Bellas Artes – gave me a privileged view of the ancient postal palace – the main post office known as Palacio de Correos – but between both majestic buildings was a clogged river of hysterical cars and buses that were going nowhere. The road had transformed into a metaphor for the country, and it made me angry. The dirty, threadbare curtain that reminded me of my old school did nothing to protect me from the chaos. I felt compressed between the traffic disaster and the sounds coming from the hallway. *How am I going to get into character like this?*

Some of my fellow artists tend to laugh and talk without rest until the last moment. They trust that it all depends on one's voice and swear that "the rest is more a pose than anything else." In fact, some of them were right out-side my door, acting like everything was okay, like there was nothing to be nervous about, but I have never once felt calm before coming out to do a scene.

The night before a debut, I have nightmares. As soon as I close my eyes, I lose my voice; I cannot fill the entire hall with it; I forget the lyrics; I sing out of tune. Just like children who don't tire of watching the same film, it seems that I do not tire of suffering the same oneiric disasters. I then rise in the middle of the night and review the music, the text, and the scenic gestures until my head pulses with pain. And it is even worse when I have to sing in a language I do not understand: the dictionary, and the language's phonology and rhythm consume all my attention. I study and review without pause: I listen to records and tape myself to compare both until I have perfected the sound as much as possible, ensuring that the song flows through my body with the ease of blood coursing through veins, that my words do not falter but dance with the music. Yet even so, I feel the same fear as if I had never rehearsed. I think I also managed to write that down in the interview. I remember that upon finishing the sentence I raised my eyes to the mirror and felt a flash of pride: I had done such a wonderful job with my makeup that no one – except Faustina, who had seen me arrive – had seen the mask-like circles under my eyes. Perhaps Rodrigo . . . although after such a long time, who knows?

I continued vocalizing, perfecting the difficult passages while obsessively fidgeting with my skirt. Outside my door, I could hear my companions laughing, going from one dressing room to the other with an enthusiasm that I found incomprehensible, impossible to share. *Am I normal?* I smiled. *Of course not.* "No one who dresses up as someone else and sings scores in languages she barely knows to a public which mostly does not understand her – and for at least three hours at that – is normal." So Father always said.

I could hear the steps of people coming and going, and through the bevelled glass I could make out a constant parade of blurry figures. The second call stopped me in my tracks. So soon? There was a knock on the door. It was Juan José, the scene director.

"Break an arm and a leg, and even your neck, my little one."

"Thank you," I replied, relieved. "Anything else before we start?"

"Yes, enjoy your wedding," he said with joy, giving me a hug before he left. I was about to shut the door when Guido, the orchestra conductor, appeared. He had gelled his hair into a cap. Old fashioned, with an almost endearing manner affecting his words and gestures, he was one of those musicians who approach the score with more caution than passion, and he never shouted at anyone. By contrast, I have worked with extremely demanding conductors, and although their musical results are undoubtedly better, the stress begins not on the opening night but rather as soon as one is asked to be part of the cast.

"I was going to wait until you came out of this cave, but then I changed my mind and decided to come right in," said Guido. He then continued: "Don't hold back that *F* we spoke about. Remember, it is not a pause. *Va bene?*"

What a difference from those who say, "You didn't study sol-fa!" or "Shit! Why can't you remember that is not a pause?" The musicians are happy with Guido because he doesn't scold them if they play out of tune, arrive late, or are absent without notice. They say that is what is great about a permanent position within their union: no one can touch you. I admire Guido's patience. After kissing my hands, he left my room with a warm smile on his face that made me feel calmer.

Once he was gone, I looked into the mirror again. I think I may have taken up this habit so as to not feel so alone, in the same way that some people turn on the television just to hear another human's voice. The costume fit me well – and I rejoiced in the knowledge that I was the only one to wear it. It is repugnant to wear clothes that someone else has already sweat in because the crinolines and outer fabrics do not allow for cleaning. I congratulated myself because my makeup was perfect and I would not have to go to the small makeup room at the end of the hall

– not even for help with the false eyelashes. I had managed to place them where they would not obstruct my vision (quite an achievement considering I usually ruin the first pair!). I was comforted by the certainty that Rodrigo was already down in the pit amongst the second violins and would not be able to distract me. Sharing the stage with Dimitri and Elena was also soothing. I wanted desperately to be near them – to listen to the overture. "Enjoy your wedding to Figaro," I told myself in the mirror. The sudden cacophony of musicians tuning their instruments felt as rough as gravel – as though it had invaded my space through the speaker on the ceiling. *Damn speaker.* I clenched my teeth and, after a long sigh, I set to go out. Just as I put my hand on the doorknob, Tamara entered in a rush, almost colliding with me. She was followed by Faustina and Elena.

"It is urgent that I speak with you, Damiana, please."

"I told her they were about to make third call, but she stubbornly refused to listen to me," interrupted Faustina.

"I'm going to ask that they give her a ticket and walk her to a seat, so she can watch the performance," offered Elena, avoiding Tamara's eyes.

"Don't you worry about anything, Damiana. We are taking her away right now," Faustina implored.

I looked at all three of them, incredulous. "What is this? What is going on?" I focused on my sister: "Get out of here, Tamara."

She sat on the stool by the dressing table and broke into tears. It was clear that she was drunk, but it had been a long time since I had been surprised by that.

"She made a scene downstairs at the artists' entrance, and since her name was not on the guest list they wouldn't let her through. And tell me, in her state, who is going to believe that she is your relative? So the police arrived and I, by chance, noticed and came down, and . . ." Faustina began to explain.

I looked at Faustina with such impatience that she stopped dead. Silence fell like a guillotine. Outside, the instruments ceased for a moment. They would be tuning briefly under the guidance of the first violin. It was the moment before Guido walked to his podium. I imagined people in the audience getting ready for the overture: they would be shifting in their seats, some coughing like patients with terminal tuberculosis; they would have leafed through the program and maybe even learned about the plot of *The Marriage of Figaro* before turning the program into a fan. I needed to rush out of the dressing room and take my place. Susanna enters the stage as soon as the overture is over. I walked toward the door and Tamara slumped her shoulders in defeat.

She bit her lips, almost obedient, but raised her tearful eyes, wounded and whelming with sadness, and whispered in a quiet voice, "Dad is dying."

My name is Tamara. Not Tammy or anything like that. When you are not the prettiest, you have to find other ways of getting attention – like the force of the blow that your name has when you say it.

Mirrors are her enemies, and magazines conspire against her because, no matter how hard she has tried to appear on their pages, none have ever spoken of her. She's so tired she no longer seeks to erase her absence. She doesn't care that the interview in the notebook belongs to her sister. She decides to read it and, when she can, to answer as well. Under the cascade of black hair framing a face the colour of sand, a whispering voice dictates, "When your talent falls into a slumber you must set it to dream in a timeless liquor." Tequila by choice, but they're all the same. They all work when it comes to stopping thought, or to making the unimportant things hurt while hiding the things that truly matter.

She leaves the notebook on the dresser and raises her eyes to look at Damiana's dressing room. She sees the photo. *They gave me one too, and I lost it.* She is almost certain that she lost it on purpose. Why hold on to a lie printed in colour? Why remember those bell-bottomed pants as red as the blood in which her mother drowned? Even now, after so many years, Tamara still does not sleep well. Even now, she wakes up asking herself if her mother had felt pain. *My "even nows"* *are never going to end; they just whirl and bite* *each other's tails and haunt my insomnia*, she writes. She re- fuses to look at the picture again or to even remember it. It is there, but it has no permission to exist.

She doesn't know why she came looking for Damiana. Why today, precisely? *After waiting so long, you could have* *waited another day.* That is not true. She wants to leave but is afraid. She can't stand the idea of being alone when Eusebio Guerra dies. *If you die, Father…* Death is even more unjust when there is no one to share it with. It is a relief to drop her weight on other shoulders. But Tamara feels bad because she knows she will listen to Damiana's voice bent and breaking under the words that Tamara has burdened her with, dragging herself through the music as if through mud. She vomits.

After, while she prowls the room, inhaling the aromat- ic lotions in Damiana's jars and caressing the costumes in the closet, Tamara thinks about Faustina. About how Faustina has never liked her, and that is why she takes great pleasure in making her angry. *I wonder if she knows what* *an orgasm is.* She doubts it, because no one who does could be as meddlesome and sour-faced. *Not even the most* *desperate man in the world would like to see Faustina com-* *ing, spilling her watery humanity over him.* Suddenly Faustina opens the door. She looks at Tamara with instinc- tive mistrust – and then disgust. A sour smell has invaded everything. It is only then that Tamara becomes aware of it, and she opens the window. The noise of the cars on the avenue assails her and combines with the sudden sound of water. Faustina is rinsing out Damiana's sink, creating a bridge with her arms as long as she can to separate herself from the remnants of that breakfast-lunch-dinner-in-one. Tamara feels like asking her, "Have you thought that your autobiography should be entitled *The Badly Fucked One?*" – but holds herself back. She seeks refuge in the ink.

I no longer feel like fighting. Yesterday, she didn't either. In truth, for a long time now, she only says things in writing, in silence, or singing in complicity with some jukebox. She breathes her own words, is her own echo and receptor. *It's been a long time since I've had someone to talk to, because Dad doesn't listen and because everyone has left.* The sound of the music coming from the stage and the noise of the cars in the street crash like waves in the air. It is hard to breathe. Tamara turns the page in the notebook and begins to read, but the photo distracts her. She squeezes her eyes to stop seeing it. To forget.

Faustina slams the door on her way out.

 CR&D

TELL US ABOUT YOUR FAMILY
I have two siblings, Tamara and Eduardo. I am the oldest.
Due to the occupations each one of us has, we have not
seen each other for a while.

Why did I agree to respond to this? I didn't know that Marilú would dare ask me about my family life, although I should have guessed. Even then, I thought she would have focused more on my career. That is how Elena promised it would be. How could I begin to explain everything? The truth is that Tamara, Eduardo, and I couldn't be more different. It is not only a matter of physical appearance. Of least importance is the fact that she looks more like Father, I like Mother, and, that in Eduardo's features, the best characteristics of both of our parents should find such unbearable harmony. If someone stopped to look at us closely, he would conclude that, in fact, the only thing gathering us in the same family is our shared last name. Also, perhaps, at times, our gestures. At least, that's how it used to be. I no longer knew. I had to consider my answer.

Tamara was always restless. Brave. When we were girls she would trap insects to inspect them – and then scare others. Especially me.

I remember that Eduardo would watch our arguments with indifference – an indifference that stayed with him and was still sharp in his eyes the last time we were together. Many of those times, after Mother was gone, I felt the desire to strike Tamara to get Eduardo's attention – to make him pay us heed. Curiously, I never considered hitting him. He seemed so small compared to me. I had not noticed that he and I were parallel lines. How many years passed before I dared to slap Tamara? By then, our brother had already surpassed me even in that.

A MEMORY FROM YOUR ADOLESCENCE
What way is this to ask questions, without question marks or anything? Is this how you write for school, Marilú?

I made an effort to not seem like Father, to not be more annoyed than necessary, and I replied:

Perhaps your Aunt Elena has already told you about this. The first time I got drunk was with my sister, when she had just turned seventeen. Father was on a trip, and we felt so free. But the next day I woke up so dizzy that I never drank again. Besides, by that point I was taking singing lessons and I had to take care of my voice. And thus I was a very calm adolescent.

Not like my sister. Why do I remember these things? I don't like noticing that I have not forgotten anything.

"So what, then, shall we celebrate?" asked Tamara, smiling.

"You tell me what you want to do." I knew she had something in mind. Her eyes gave her away.

"I brought a locksmith to open Dad's wine cellar and make me copies of the key."

I was about to reprimand her, but she would not allow me to give my opinion. "Do you want to have fun or what? You wait here. The man said he wouldn't take long at all."

It was hard not to follow her, but I did not want to be her accomplice. I tried to busy myself by leafing through a magazine. I recall that Tamara was right – the locksmith was indeed fast.

"Dare to deny that I am brilliant!" She burst into the living room, laughing, and showed me the bottle she had just stolen.

"We'll be caught."

"The new key is very similar to the old one, so Dad won't notice. Besides, nothing is going to happen if you keep quiet and tomorrow you give me some money to buy another bottle."

Tamara showed me the bottle like a pirate showing off his treasure. It was impossible not to smile – and even harder to refuse her offer. She lit one cigarette after another as we talked, and I remember the surprise I felt at watching her smoke. *When did you grow up so much, Tamara?* Mysterious behind the curtain of smoke, sole owner of the smoke rings that floated above her face like ghosts. I wanted to ask her about Eduardo. She raised her chin in a gesture of disdain, exhaled a geyser of smoke that made me cough, and then said jokingly: "Fucking kid. It would have been so easy to drown him in Caracas when he was little."

We had not mentioned that city in a long time. When anyone asks, we say Venezuela, not Caracas. That word – the entire city – disappeared for us three at the same time mother did. What is not pronounced does not exist, and I think that we always strove to believe that pain will vanish if it has no sound or definition or place of origin or words that lend it weight. Tamara flinched in realization that she had uttered the forbidden word and changed the topic immediately. I should have stopped her. It would have been a good opportunity, the only one, the last one perhaps, to return together to that silenced road and to give it words. But as usual, Tamara was quicker and more audacious.

"Do you know how I can tell if I like someone or not?" she asked me with an already blurred voice. I shook my head. "I imagine them having an orgasm. If I don't feel like throwing up, I like them."

Tamara had always wanted to be an actress.

"We have had enough of your sister set on living like a gypsy. Choose a decent profession. Actors are promiscuous and illiterate," Father answered her.

I had kept quiet. In many cases, singers are not very cultured either, but music disguises this with a certain dignity. (That is something I had written down in the interview. *I was lucky because Father made us read one book per week and give him a written report. If it wasn't perfectly written, he wouldn't let us go out on the weekend or watch TV. We had to work on the report until it was flawless.*) Tamara's real problem in becoming an actress was that she had Eusebio Guerra's face. From the beginning, she was warned that her talent was not sufficient for a successful career, and she continually expressed her desire to submit herself to plastic surgery and treatments that might improve her chances of success. Just in case, Father cancelled Tamara's credit card and shut down the whole subject in one fell swoop.

"I am going to find myself a producer. That is my plan. That's where I'm at. And you?"

"I don't know any producers."

"Don't pretend you don't understand what I mean. You are going out with someone."

"When would I do that?" I lied and blushed so that Tamara noticed. "Can't you see that I am at the Conservatory all the time?"

"Yes, but not conserving your virginity, right?"

I guess that my laughter gave me away.

"You'll tell me right now! Why haven't you told me anything?"

Oh, Tamara. As if things were spoken aloud in our family.

"His name is Rodrigo. He is a violinist."

I shouldn't have told her. It was the tequila. Tamara questioned me at will and asked to meet him. We were talking at our most enthusiastic, when Eduardo walked in and noticed we were drinking. Tamara, sitting next to me on the living room floor, held the almost empty bottle in her hand. Her unsteady wave of greeting inopportunely set him off.

"Where did you get that bottle?"

"Where do you think, little brain?" Tamara answered. "We are celebrating. Why don't you do us a favour and fuck off somewhere else?"

"Why don't you do yourself a favour and stop talking like a tramp?"

Between my amazement and my dizziness, Eduardo appeared enormous. He spoke just like Father and was almost as threatening, but at his age . . .

"You both know that if Father is not home I am in charge. I am not a man for nothing." And he turned to look at me: "You should have a look at your face. What a shame."

I couldn't look at him. In contrast, Tamara confronted him. "If Dad is not home, no one is in charge, least of all you."

Tamara looked like a chihuahua trying to frighten a pit bull. Eduardo slapped her. I recall the burning sensation I felt suddenly at the certainty of having witnessed the same scene many times before, when Father would hit Mother. Perhaps Eduardo and Tamara remembered too, because the silence that followed the slap was all the more violent. We were quiet for a few seconds before reacting. Was that the first time I noticed that particular absence in our eyes, the absence of life that still shone in the old photograph? I was not sure.

"Take some aspirin," Eduardo said before locking himself in his room, "or you won't even be able to get up tomorrow."

Of course, we didn't listen.

The next day, I had such a terrible headache that I promised myself never to drink again. Tamara chose the opposite. She would not be intimidated. Besides, neither Father nor Eduardo knew about the key and I never wanted to betray my sister's trust by telling them. At first, I replaced the missing bottles. Later, she found ways to come across others.

From that point on, everything was different. All we had in common were our last name, some similar gestures, and memories neither of us ever wanted to speak of.

What could I actually write for Marilú, to complete my answer?

We lived in many different places because my father was the Mexican ambassador to different countries, but we returned to Mexico after my mother's death, and I remained here until I won a scholarship to continue my studies in Paris.

❧ 2 ❧

I felt as if the rat swimming in circles inside me had suddenly exploded; as if my body were breaking. I could not articulate the words to ask Tamara where Father was, or what had happened. Nor could I ask her if Eduardo already knew. There was no time to find my fleeting voice because just then they announced "Third call, third call," and someone rushed in to say to us "*In bocca al luppo,*" and someone else responded "*Creppi il lupo*" and I thought, *Yes, I am indeed walking toward the wolf's mouth,* but that, even if my life depended on it, I would not be able to slay the wolf. An unfamiliar face suddenly approached and asked us to get closer to the stage. None of the orchestra musicians could be seen. Only the technicians, singing to themselves, walked freely from one place to another. In my trajectory from the dressing room I had spotted a few "sneaks" who avidly peeked toward the stage, thinking that they would get a better view even though there was nothing to see behind the closed curtain – I've never understood why some people, usually friends of cast members, prefer to watch a performance from backstage, instead of sitting comfortably in the theatre. I thought it bizarre for me to have noticed, never before paying attention to who was walking around the stage. Why did I notice it in this instance? To escape? To acknowledge that what Tamara told me was true? That it was really happening?

Applause rained down like arrows from the hall, weakening me further. Guido prepared himself to begin the overture. I still could not manage to make a sound. I found myself incapable of protest and had no strength to ask anything. I covered my stomach with my arms because suddenly my body was in the way and everything ached. I walked in step with my fellow singers, a prisoner to an undercurrent, allowing myself to be led so as not to drown. With me was the memory of Tamara's perfume, the one from always. The one that Mother had used.

Elena, now turned into Cherubino, wanted to cheer me up: "Susanna, you cannot be sad! It's your wedding to Figaro – you must trust that everything will be all right!" Dimitri came near and took me by the waist. There was no need for words.

I wanted to ask, "Dying of what, Tamara," and "why, precisely, today, Father?" But my throat made no sound and I could not escape because those strong Russian arms, so beloved, held me tight and because Elena was right. If I were to write about that night, I'd certainly be able to say that I had never felt so helpless, so miserable, so sad, and so furious. No one word is enough. *How long since I have seen you, Eusebio Guerra?* For a moment it seemed like no time had passed at all, except that Rodrigo, in the orchestra pit, was now sitting among the second violins. I had to struggle to recognize myself: such an alien, voluminous dress, my face pancaked in makeup, my eyes decorated with cow-like lashes, my body a ceramic figurine held together by chewing gum.

When my fellow singers said it again, with what I thought was more sympathy than affection – "In bocca al luppo" – and Elena kissed my cheek and Dimitri let go, beaming like a true Figaro – "*Andiamo*" – and guided me behind the curtain to a chair where the beginning of my scene was marked, I did not even remember that this was the first time I had led a cast in my own country. The only thing I could think was, *You'd better not die without seeing me, Father. Don't you dare die while I sing.*

CRObO

Perhaps everything had started with the dress. Ever since the costume designer – daughter of a famous painter and someone whom no one dared openly contradict – ordered that Susanna wear different shades of purple throughout the course of the opera, one disaster after another coiled together in a rope that threatened to strangle us all. Marisita, the choir director – a retired soprano with a disposition as sour as her breath – turned out to be extremely superstitious. She reminded us that at the Bastille Opera, the stage manager had prohibited the colour green (bad luck in France), and demanded that here we do the same with purple because it was bad luck in Italy and her late father was Italian. She was emphatic, as if educating us, that on those stages no one wearing even a green tie or a purple scarf was allowed to walk. She, who had never sung in either France or Italy! So, no green and no purple. Until the colours of the costumes were changed, she refused to cooperate.

I later learned that the timpanist of the orchestra had joined her in her protest. He asked for a replacement. The rest of the musicians backed him up. At least he had been candid enough to communicate his intention to withdraw, and for that alone he deserved some recognition. "After all," people said, "he could have called in sick on opening night." It would not have been the first time someone had abruptly left the orchestra without a replacement.

The timpanist became some kind of leader. Other small protests ensued, with one technician – a man who spoke perfect Italian – saying that those in the choir "might just organize a bigger protest," as that is what they love to do, "with banners and all" (which is why the shiny lilac dresses that had been suggested for the women were definitively cancelled). I would've found all this hard to believe had I not seen it unfold.

But not everyone was actively involved in protesting. There were also other musicians who carried on unperturbed. With the TV on a sports channel, or immersed in some discreet headphones, they were present only in body – just as I was at that union meeting I had attended out of mere curiosity, the one where I found all this out. I had remained at the back of the room so no one would see me and drum me out before I decided to leave of my own accord. I didn't share the superstition about the purple, and I did not want to predispose myself against the entire choir just because of Marisita's attitude. Truthfully, I didn't care a straw what colour they wore, so I left the room in silence. I was so eager to sing – so excited to be Susanna – that I would have worn any colour asked of me. Besides, the famous painter and my father had been friends for quite a long time.

I recalled this in a lightning's flash as Dimitri and I settled in behind the curtain to begin the *duettino*. There I was, about to sing, "*Guarda un po, mio caro Figaro, Guarda adesso il mio capello*," thinking about Father and Tamara, about the director of the choir and the timpanist, and irreparably stuck in the bad luck – purple – dress. The budget had only allowed for the choir's costumes to be redone. Three more dresses awaited me in the dressing room – two of them in shades of mauve and lilac.

I was so engrossed that I missed my starting point. Dimitri just looked at me, perplexed. His eyes appeared even more immense with the makeup, but he continued as if nothing had happened. I caught up with him a few beats later. Because Guido marked the exact entry point with his baton and I could see the alarm in his gesture, I was sure that every member of the public had noticed my mistake. This further intimidated me. Susanna's flirting, her confidence, her joy before the wedding – all of it seemed impossible. I am not exactly sure when – after the dialogue of the bells? – Dimitri softly guided me to the sofa where we'd begun, on stage right. He stood at my side, playing with my hair without letting go of my hand, and so we finished the scene as best we could. When at last he took me by the waist to make our exit, I had the certainty that the "*Coraggio, mio tesoro*" he sang before he saw me vanish were the three most sincere words I had heard in my life.

Cherubino waited for me backstage, but I wanted to see no one. If I let anyone hug me, I would not be able to continue. I gestured him/her to go, and settled behind the scenery to let the scenes (happily, without me) play out. There were still two arias, another duet with Figaro, duets with Marcellina, Cherubino, the Count, and the Countess, one trio with the Count and Basilio and one with the Count and Countess, the sextet and the three finals to go. The scenes surged through my mind like an avalanche. At the start, Susanna runs into all the characters; she is trapped. I remembered Guido's instructions to be the strongest voice at the end of the second act – to find the perfect balance so as not to shout but to be the strongest all the same. Juan José's insistence that I imbue Susanna with extreme sensuality and audacity felt inconceivable. If I went on like this, I would ruin everyone's work. The critics would tear me apart. I would never have another contract. To live without singing? The mere possibility left me breathless. Surely, in the first few rows, the terrible little bald man from the *Informador* would be seated. He always shows up, score in hand and, with the help of a flashlight, notes every mistake in order to make the most precise denunciation. *Father, what is happening to you?* I could not hold my tears any longer. I leaned forward so as to allow them to fall straight down and not ruin my makeup.

Someone – I don't know who – placed a glass of water, a box of tissues, and a hand mirror next to me. I remained silent but was infinitely thankful. When I heard the scene with Marcellina and Bartolo progressing without problems and knew that soon I would have to return to the stage, I stopped my tears, stood up straight, checked my eyeliner, and walked to the spot where I would make my entrance. My eyes were reddened, but I didn't care. I was not going to think about Father or Tamara or my bad start. I had to stop my voice from sounding weak. I could not sing out of time. I drank the water and waited patiently. Marcellina exited the stage and, without making eye contact, we stood together and waited for Bartolo to finish his aria so we could step out of the wings. Once I stood facing my fictional love rival under the bright lights, it was as if everything was really happening for the first time. The colour of her dress caught my attention. Blue! I hadn't noticed. It made me so angry that it helped me push the scene of flying insults forward. The public laughed. "*Sibilla decrepita, da rider mi fa,*" I sang with pleasure. I wasn't angry just with her character who so cunningly wanted to steal my Dimitri, I was angry with *whatshername* because it was me – not Marcellina – wearing the purple dress.

The rest of the arias played out quickly. When I made my exit at the end of my final scene, I felt calmer. Figaro was in charge of the last scene in the first act. He was still singing when I walked into my dressing room. Waiting for me were Tamara, Faustina, and Elena.

"Quick, Faustina, hand me my other dress," I said, trying not to look at Tamara.

When the public began to applaud with force and to shout "Bravo," I was not surprised. Dimitri had been outstanding the entire time, and like never before. I went into the bathroom to don my dress. The air was sour with vomit. A glass streaked with the remnants of Alka-Seltzer sat by the sink. Tamara always left a trail.

"Why don't you go out and say thanks, Elena?" I shouted through the door.

"We agreed not to go out between acts. Juan told us to wait until the end."

The zipper on my dress jammed, but I didn't want to ask for help fixing it. I didn't want to meet anyone's eyes.

The only place I felt safe was in that bathroom – even though it smelled of rancid tequila. *Should I ask about Father, or wait until the end of the performance? Can I be patient? Will I be able to go on singing if I know all the details?* I heard some small knocks on the door and Tamara's voice, as if she had read my mind.

"Do you want me to talk to you, Damiana, or would you prefer to wait?"

I stopped completely. I held my breath. I didn't know what to answer. My silence worked as a signal for Tamara to continue, and I breathed out little by little while I listened to her.

"He began to feel weak. It was an effort to move. First a clumsy leg, you see? But nothing too serious. Then an arm with some stiffness. The next day neither his arms nor his legs responded well. He didn't want to go see a doctor; he attributed it all to working too much. You know what he's like. But suddenly he couldn't breathe well, and that is when I took him to the hospital. He is in intensive care. Connected to a respirator."

She opened the bathroom door and peered in. Her eyes were like broken glass. "Can I wait here? I am afraid to be alone there with him."

I closed my eyes and shook my head at the image of Father assaulted by tubes. I understood my sister's fear. *What will I do if you die in front of me, Father?* I nodded. *Stay, Tamara.* Then I heard Juan José's voice and his nasal question. Luckily, Tamara closed the bathroom door quickly. *No, Juan, of course I'm not well, why do you ask such stupid questions?*

"Of course I'm fine, Juan. I'm perfectly fine. Don't worry. Of course I can go on."

"You will see that everything will work out fine, my queen," he lied, trying to soothe me.

It was clear that he was a bit drunk, but not as much as Tamara had been when she arrived. I found it strange that he spoke so sweetly to me. He had always been prone to anger, especially if things didn't work out perfectly. Dimitri and I had disobeyed his signal in the first scene, and I had made a disaster of the beginning. Sensing that Juan José felt pity for me rather than anger made me feel indignant. But I decided to wait. I didn't have the energy to enter into any argument. I was finally able to fasten my dress. I checked myself in the mirror and breathed deeply once more. From behind the door, there came a silence that made me relax. I thought they had all had a glimmer of sublime intelligence and abandoned the room. I was just beginning to enjoy the peace when Rodrigo's voice interrupted.

"Damiana, it's me." There were two more little knocks on the plywood door. "Damiana, please open."

I didn't want to answer.

Not caring, he persisted until Faustina stepped in. "Why don't you stop your 'Damiana this' and 'Damiana that' and wait like a good boy till the show is over? Besides, isn't it time for you to return to your pit?"

What a piece of work, Faustina, I thought, almost wanting to laugh. But I held it in and waited until I thought that Rodrigo was gone. I came out of the bathroom ready to continue, buoyed by my second costume and a second wind. I was about to head toward the stage to take my place next to Elena when Tamara stopped me with a hand on my shoulder.

"Forgive me," she murmured.

I knew from the tone of her voice that she wasn't referring solely to tonight's incident. She was offering me old apologies with such a new and transparent sincerity that I was thrown off. I didn't know what to say to her or how to react. Tamara smiled, even though she was beginning to cry again. Then she even winked at me like she used to when we were little. Rodrigo, who had already moved away from the door, chose that moment to leave.

I could hear the familiar comings and goings as the stagehands changed scenery and the orchestra tuned their instruments once again. "How's the soccer match going?" inquired a voice. "One-zero, the Chivas are winning." I don't know why this fact cheered me up. Michaela, who was playing the Countess and who would not speak from the day before she was to sing in order to protect her voice, came toward me and gave me a silent embrace. I let myself be carried by a tide of technicians, extras, "gatecrashers" – a whole regiment marching the corridor near the door that displayed my name in that ugly calligraphy I refused to look at. I still had many questions on my mind, questions that I really needed to stop thinking about. For example: *What is worse – to feel youself asphyxiating or to suddenly know that someone is going to kill you?*

The second call fell like a whip on my back. *When did they make the first call?* Before going down to the orchestra pit, Guido approached me briefly. He told me not to worry, that he would be keeping an eye on me the whole time. All I had to do, he said, was to follow him. I nodded, thankful. Faustina had surely been in charge of spreading the news about Father as quickly as possible in order to protect me, but I was not able to thank her. I felt even more exposed – almost naked. I was holding Elena's hand, but I felt like hiding behind her. Dimitri joined us then. He took me by the arm and began to play with my hair, softly rubbing the back of my head. Flanked by them, I thought with conviction: *Ultimately, the purple dress is quite pretty. That Marisita and the timpanist can go fuck themselves.*

☙❧

Tamara, waiting alone in Damiana's dressing room, takes off her shoes. Out of everyone in the family, she has the ugliest feet. *Not even Dad's are like this.* She knows because, since he fell ill, she has been massaging his feet with oil. She has chosen to lie to Damiana. She is not brave enough to tell her that their Father has been sick for weeks. Tamara looks at her feet and tries to visualize Eduardo's. His look like women's feet. Were they not covered in hair, he could don an elegant pair of high heels. *It's strange*, she thinks, *that my brother and I have so many attributes that are opposite to what they should be.* She examines her Goofy-like toes and concludes ruefully that her brother's feet could be Cinderella's. Immediately, she curses herself because her most intimate analogies always end up having to do with Disney. Even Damiana's face resembles Bambi. She writes: *Children who have lost mothers remain Bambi-esque forever.* But Tamara is unable to find signs of a fawn-like sweetness in her own face. She recalls that Damiana always paints her toenails, that she doesn't mind that they look like round, colourful candies. *What colour are you wearing now? Do you remember how Mom used to play with our feet when we were children?* She would like to ask her, but she inhales only doubt. She wants to melt into the little sofa; it alone receives her with open arms. She wants to cover her ears and stop the path of Rodrigo's voice toward her head; she wants her hands to be unbreachable barriers. She wants a drink. She doesn't know what she was thinking when she came here. *I can't remember what your feet are like, Rodrigo.* His voice calling Damiana drills a hole into Tamara's stomach.

A Happy Childhood Memory

My response was immediate. I didn't have to think about it for a second:

The Sugus races. We loved Sugus candies. Father, Ed-
uardo, Tamara, and I would pile the candies into really
tall towers and then cram them in our mouths. It was a
sacred ritual. Usually in the evening, the four of us would
sit on the living room carpet, circled around the bag, and
reach in for several candies. Each of us had a favourite
flavour, but we were allowed to mix them up. We avidly
unwrapped them, but with care because part of the fun
was to avoid tearing the little wrappers. We fashioned
small hills of multi-coloured paper, constructed our sand-
wiches, (Father's purple, Tamara's red and yellow,
Eduardo's green, and mine blue-white or orange) and ate
them in one gulp. The one who could fit the most candies
into his or her mouth and swallow them the quickest was
the winner.

It goes without saying it was hard to eat so many soft candies all at once. Our cheeks could barely hold them. Mother would get angry because she could see the crushed sweets between our teeth. "You look like cavemen," she'd say. She did not like the Sugus races. Father said that it was because "Russians don't have a sense of humour." She would protest: "On top of being in bad taste, they are dangerous. The children are going to choke, thanks to you, Eusebio." Father would shrug and open his mouth as wide as possible to show his purple tongue and the clotted mass of half-melted sweets. Mother would get angrier and we would laugh. "In the end, it's you who pays for the dentist," she would conclude before leaving us. "I am always the one who pays for everything," Father would shout. But you couldn't always understand the words because his mouth was full.

Tamara and Father always won these contests. Eduardo needed help unwrapping the Sugus: his young fingers were not yet nimble. Father would get Eduardo's candies ready to give him an advantage. Then Father and Tamara would build and devour their towers at great speed. I never managed to catch up to them. I didn't like the coloured saliva to slide down my chin. I felt ashamed. I also felt a bit guilty for making Mother angry. How could I have imagined then that my guilt would get worse – because she died before I could apologize and tell her she was right, tell her how much I needed her.

My siblings did not attend our mother's wake. Nor the burial the following day. Father thought they were too young.

Only I went with him. I remember four candles in the brown room, the silver box in the centre, the lid closed so that no one could see what had happened to her face. I have never known which is worse: what I imagine hidden in that box or what I would have seen had I opened it. If, in her interview, Marilú had asked about my favourite animal, I would have answered "elephants" without hesitation. In a television program, I saw dying elephants rub themselves against the bones of their dead to choose the place where they will rest forever. Because, in life, they touch each other so often, they can recognize members of their family through close contact with their remains. They then lie down beside the bones and allow for nature to slowly reunite them. Time does not let elephants forget what the bodies of their loved ones were like. That is why they are my favourite animal. Because I long to have known my mother in this way. Because I would have liked to have kept her hand to compare it with mine as I grew, or perhaps her foot, to look in depth at her cheery toes. Elephants are my favourite animals, but I am also envious of them; I will never be able to go snuggle next to my mother in order to die less alone.

Marilú's question was in reference to a happy memory from childhood. I don't know why I recalled the worst one as well. The one that made others lose their meaning. I remember great wreaths and arrangements of white flowers. People sitting on sofas or standing in small clusters, breaking the silence with whispers in that Caribbean accent I had found so hard to understand when we first arrived, but which my mother liked so much . . . I remember that the air smelled like the sea salt, and felt like warm wax, the breeze sticky. I wouldn't let go of Father's hand, or his blazer. I had never searched for his proximity with such eagerness. He must have noticed. Some people told him that I shouldn't be there at all, that I was too little to understand. I have always hated that adult habit of speaking about children as if they were not present. Father shook his head, hugged me, and remained silent. He knew that leaving me alone would have been worse. One of his best qualities was his ability to guess without having to be told. That is why he allowed me to crumple a corner of his blazer all day long. That is why, when we stood in front of the hole that was about to swallow my mother in her shiny silver container, he held me against his breast so that I would see nothing. The sound of shovels scraping the ground, lifting up earth and throwing it over empty space – no – over my mother . . . This sound overwhelmed everything else. The shovels against the earth, the moist soil falling on metal, and the constant din of the Caracas cicadas together composed a requiem. One stops noticing cicadas until suddenly it seems like they are screaming, just as when one turns up the volume to something that, though playing all along, had been forgotten. That morning, with the sun beating down on us, the sound of the cicadas was inscribed like a tattoo on my ears. Since then, I cannot recall Mother's voice – not her laughter, her shouts, not even her calling us "cavemen." Her words are mute. Only her flute makes a sound. And my dad's breathing, his hands cupping my head to his chest, acting like a helmet – one that was unable to protect me.

Ever since that day, blue skies and sunny days make me sad. My life changed on a beautiful day, and nothing in the sky altered to reflect my loss. That will always seem unfair to me. I cheer up when it rains: people who suffer on those days can at least be consoled thinking that the sky is with them in their grief.

Until that day, death, for me, was Georgina – my turtle. We found her one morning, stiff and milky-eyed. We never saw Georgina again. Mother bought us another turtle which we immediately named Leonora in honour of Beethoven's opera. Leonora was still alive the day we buried Mother. Now that Mother was dead, I asked myself if someone else would replace her, just like Leonora had taken Georgina's place. I asked myself what my sister would say when she found out. How Eduardo would react to Mother's permanent absence. I asked myself if, in truth, we would never see her again. The void was impossible to understand. I couldn't believe that Mother would never again play with us. No more hide-and-seek games with her and Father. And never again would Mother pick up Sugus wrappers with her toes.

I had to shake my head to clear my thoughts. If I didn't move on to the next question I was going to become very sad.

How Did You Begin to Sing

My mother played the flute, and for a while she played in a local orchestra where we lived. She loved music. She took me to the opera for the first time. She taught me to love music.

I reread my entry with satisfaction. It sounded good despite not being entirely true.

When we returned from Mother's burial, Father called Tamara and Eduardo and the four of us met in his study. I don't remember his exact words, instead of saying that she had been killed, he said that she died, and from then on, I did the same. Days passed and Mother's things remained in place. We did not return to school because Father had begun to organize our departure from Venezuela. He hired a private tutor so that we would not lose the school year, and he was content with that. None of us asked questions, probably because we knew that Father would say nothing more. Mother's portrait still hung on the wall. It was the only thing that spoke of her. It was impossible to sleep. All three of us cried at night, but only Eduardo and Tamara managed to fall asleep out of exhaustion. Headaches forced me to get up and flee from bed, to wish I could turn into dust so I could vanish. Father wandered the house all through the night, and I could hear his footsteps everywhere, dragging along with the desolation of someone who is tired, lost. He would enter our bedrooms stealthily and stand a long while at the foot of our beds. It made me scared. I would only get up once he had left. I didn't know what he was looking for. I began to follow him. I'd watch his movements without him noticing.

One night, after stopping in all three bedrooms, he sat down in the living room. While I watched him, I made a wish. I asked with all my heart that everything return to how it had been, so I could remember Mother's voice. I swore that I wouldn't care about the shouts and the blows. I wouldn't even mind repeating that afternoon in which Mother begged, "Not in front of the children, please." Nothing stopped me from wishing time would turn back. In truth, it was not necessary to witness those scenes to know how much those slaps hurt. Father had large hands.

Whenever we heard the warning, Tamara and I would hide behind the door, or hide under the bed, embracing each other.

It usually began: "Stop playing that fucking flute, I've had it with your constant tooting."

This would almost always be followed by: ". . . I'm almost finished."

And then: "I told you to shut up. I'm going to break your hands with that thing to make you understand."

And one day: "I've never hit you, and you've hit me three times now. Please forgive me, Eusebio."

And another day: "No more, please, no more."

Almost every day.

There was also the sound of objects hitting the floor or the walls. Smashing. And the smell of sweat. And the salt of tears. Torn clothes, stained with a deep red that sometimes did not wash out. Once, from a slap, some little decorative stones flew from my mother's glasses. Tamara and I had always loved those glasses. Our mother looked beautiful in them. We scoured the carpet for hours to find the little coloured stones one by one, so that our mother could stick them back in place. But the frames were hopelessly twisted, and she was never able to wear them again outside the house. She would only put them on for us, and she would let us play with them.

After that, Tamara began to confront Father.

"Leave her alone, Dad! Let go of her. Don't be a bully."

"Get out of the way, Tamara! This is not children's business," and he'd push her.

"Don't you touch my daughter," and Mother would throw herself at him to defend Tamara.

In the end, Father would apologize to both of them, and then lock himself with Tamara in his study. Who knows what things he said to her? Mother and I, with Eduardo in her arms, would walk away when the quarrel ended. My sister always came out of there ready to eat towers of Sugus and play as if nothing had happened. By contrast, I found it difficult to forgive him. I ended up doing so, but not willingly. He would be diligent and sweet for the next few days, and Mother would insist that we not hold a grudge. I never really understood why Father was so aggressive. I also didn't know why Mother put up with him for so long, why she didn't do something to save herself.

But after her death I clearly understood that anything was better than this new silence, even the blows and screams. Anything, in order to have her back.

Every sentence I recalled Mother saying was still formed of soundless words the night I secretly followed Father to the living room. Again, I wished in my heart that everything be as before. But as though in immediate response – crushing any possibility that my wish might come true – Father rose to his feet, retrieved the bag of Sugus from the cupboard drawer, walked decisively to the kitchen, and with rage threw the candy into the garbage. He didn't really comment on it the next day, nor the day after. Only that we had to take better care of our teeth. None of us dared protest, nor did we ever propose to play again, even when we were alone. I have not eaten a single Sugus since.

The next day, so I wouldn't forget the sound of Mother's flute, I began to use my voice to imitate the scales which she used to practice. The melodies she played. At least that was going to remain with me. No one was going to be able to take it away. It was the best way to suffocate so much silence, and breathe again. My cold, green Leonora stretched her neck fully to listen. That is how I began to sing.

CRBO

Tamara listens to the applause and notices that it feels different from the kind she knew in the theatre. The whole process behind the operatic stage is different. The singers do not kick objects or throw things against the floor in order to recreate a sensation of anger or some other feeling in their guts. Such a flammable state would corrode the singer's breathing before he or she stepped onstage. *It's not that all actors lose control*, she writes. But she remembers that for her to insert the characters into her body, this outburst was indispensable. She also recalls she was not the only one. In her last drama, a fellow actress so completely wrecked a wall by throwing chairs at it that she had to pay for the repairs in installments: even though she had won the most important theatre prize for her role, and even though every weekend she filled the theatre with people who came especially to see her, she didn't have the money to pay for the repairs all at once. To justify her actions, and only half in jest, she said that the dressing rooms had walls like those of a soap opera set and that is why they were all so feeble. Tamara remembers the sound of the crashes, the crushed chairs (*Who paid for those?*) – and she thinks that it was worth it because the current that took over the stage was absolutely electrifying.

Perhaps she should have followed in her colleague's footsteps, she reflects. *How long ago was that?* She counts the months while she flips through the pages of Damiana's notebook. Then she comes across the question, *A HAPPY CHILDHOOD MEMORY*.

Without trying, Tamara's mind travels back to years of being lulled to sleep by the song of cicadas. The years of marine heat clinging to skin. *Caracas, damn*. It is not a happy memory, but it is the first one to come. Christmas. There were no guests, it was only the five of them so she gave four gifts: one for Dad, one for Mom, one for Damiana and the last one for Eduardo. Her savings were enough to provide a small present for each, but she doesn't recall what those presents were – just the fact that she didn't want to forget anyone. It hurts to remember because the only thing that flies like a projectile toward her memory is the image of the porcelain dogs that little Eduardo bought for his parents. He didn't bother to get anything for his sisters because that would have prevented him from buying "something really nice" for his mom and dad, or he had said something to that effect. With utter precision, she only remembers the words of Eusebio Guerra. "You see, Tamara, your brother knows how to give good gifts. Being so intelligent, you should know that there is nothing worse than giving cheap presents. I am doing this for your own good." And right then, he picked up all the little gifts and threw them into the large garbage can in the kitchen that she'd not forgotten was blue. He then placed the little dogs from Lalito (as the family had affectionately nicknamed her brother) on a bookshelf. She remembers that she broke into tears and ran to her room. Mom tried to run after her, but the threatening hand Eusebio Guerra held high, prevented her from doing so. It was he who followed Tamara to her room and convinced her to come down again. *What did he say to me? What did you tell me, Dad, that I forgave you?*

After that, the only thing that Tamara remembers is her everlasting hatred of Christmas, and the immense disdain she feels for inexpensive gifts – except for the clay figures in the colourful wicker basket that Rodrigo gave her on her birthday. "It's a loaf of bread," he had said with a smile. Tamara felt like throwing the basket at his head. She restrained herself, unwrapped the small bundle, and pulled out the delicately crafted figures. And she fell in love with them immediately when he said, "It is you and me." She was the woman with lilies in her arms, and he, the barefoot man. *It was you and me,* she writes. She crosses it out. *What are your feet like, Rodrigo?* She doesn't remember, but she knows they are made from soft clay that warmed when nesting in her hands.

❧ 3 ❦

When I listened to Michaela sing the Countess' aria that opens the second act, I committed myself to keeping abolustely silent for an entire day before my next performance. I had never done it – Michaela's self-imposed ritual had always seemed excessive and presumptuous – but her voice floated in the air with such womanly angelic grace and lightness that she made me reconsider. Disillusion and love's longing slid by like caresses between beats. Her experience and technique held my attention in a way that had never occurred during rehearsals. I realized then that in none of them had she revealed her true voice. All this time she had greedily hidden it, and only now – before the public – did she unfold her gifts, as if painting a precious mural of sounds. *If she weighed a few pounds less, poor dear,* I thought to comfort myself. I was not to be outdone! And with that in mind, I stepped onstage. Guido threw me a conspiratorial look, as if in welcome, which gave me an even greater confidence.

Michaela caught me by surprise: instead of competing with me, she was generous – just as the Countess is with Susanna – and she seemed to be extending her hand with each phrase she sang. When we reached Elena's *Voi Che Sapete* it was clear that all three of us were enjoying it greatly. Cherubino, with his picaresque eyes, kept provoking us. The tenderness in Elena's voice taken together with Juan José's stage directions (which we now obeyed with utmost precision) made the scenes flow so easily that I felt a genuine pang of anxiety. *How long since you have "trembled and fluttered with love," like Cherubino?* But I did not become distracted. With smiles, we dressed Cherubino like a woman, and the scene in which we hide when the Count enters the bedroom unfolded perfectly. Perhaps the music critic, the fearsome little baldy from the *Informador,* would forgive me after all? Dimitri, with his enormous eyes and his tender and playful gestures, looked after me the whole time. My initial nervousness had dissolved in the music. A miraculous oblivion had descended, and I didn't for an instant think about Tamara or Father. Susanna was once again the master of the situation. Everything in me revolved around Dimitri – around my impending marriage to Figaro.

When I am asked why I am a singer, I reply with my other truth: that I would feel very vulnerable if I could not shelter myself in the notes that the orchestra weaves at each performance. I came to that realization the first time I went to the opera. Mother took me secretly, just the two of us, in celebration of my eighth birthday. She had purchased tickets to *Carmen*, and though we sat far back, we could see the action clearly. *Do you miss the orchestra, Mother?* (There were so many things I didn't know to ask her that night.) After the performance, we went backstage to the dressing rooms. I was able to see the sets piled up against the wings, touch the dancers' still-warm costumes, and gaze at the theatre seats from the other side of the house – the one which is now mine. Suddenly, I felt a chill. Who had sung Carmen that night? I can't forgive myself for the lapse in memory. We didn't save the program because Mother did not want Father to find it. And now, so many years later, no names sound familiar. There are none that I can connect to that production. At the opera that night, Mother whispered to me something that Maria Callas used to say: "To be a good singer, you must vibrate like a violin." So I made the effort to perceive in what way performers vibrated upon the stage. Years later, upon discovering that I could do it myself, the joy left me inconsolable. *You never got to see me sing, Mother.*

Somehow, Father found out that we had gone without his permission, and he became enraged. He locked himself in the bedroom with Mother, and Tamara, Eduardo, and I crept close to the door to listen. We shouldn't have, because his words proved more painful than the blows that we heard through the wood. "You went to meet up with that crappy little singer, right? You're a whore, like all Russian women, you beggars." A blow, then only silence. "And you dared take Damiana, to make her filthy as well." A sigh, and then Mother's voice, broken, tired, trying to explain: "We were friends, schoolmates, nothing else, so long ago . . ." And he – even more angry – "You think I'm an imbecile?" A broken plate, a drowned moan, another blow. "I don't know what I'll do one day, but you are going to regret it." And one last blow, the hardest one: Mother falling to the floor. "One day I'm going to kill you."

A few minutes passed before Father raged out of the bedroom like a beast, slamming the door behind him. He didn't even turn toward us, his children, as we cowered in the corner, weeping with fear. *You didn't have the courage to look at us, did you, Father? So now why should I have to be brave and watch you die?*

The three of us rushed to hug Mother. She had just managed to rinse her face with water. Her mouth still bled. Eduardo reached out to her with his small hand, made the same face he always made when he touched something disagreeable, and wiped his fingers instinctively on the bedspread. There – etched in blood upon the Belgian knit-work that Father loved so much – a perfect impression of that little hand. Mother raised herself slowly, horrified. Father's fury would reignite at the sight of his favourite counterpane ruined. She covered her mouth – now swollen shapeless – with a scarf and went to the kitchen for deter-gent. It was late. We knew that, out of shame, she didn't want to call the servants, although it was likely that the shouting had awoken everyone. The next day there were sure to be gossiping whispers and furtive glances of pity. I washed Lalito's hands while Mother and Tamara worked on the bedspread. Mother, her dress splattered and her face half covered and bruised, scrubbed as if for dear life – and perhaps her life really was in danger. It was the first time that I felt a real fear of losing her – it was as if someone had thrown me into a well and said that no one would ever come to retrieve me. Mother insisted, several times, that we go to bed, but we refused. Eduardo eventually fell asleep, but Tamara and I did not want to be without her. When at last she changed her clothes, we glimpsed the bruising on her back and arms. She tried to cover herself, but it was difficult for her to move. The welts made a pattern of violet flowers on her skin.

"Why is Daddy like this, Mommy?" Tamara asked. In the pause that followed I was suddenly aware of the smell of blood. Sour. Oddly metallic. *Does blood always smell like this or only when there is a lot of it?* I didn't ask Mother.

"That's the way your father is, and you must love him. He loves you very much. He loves you both – the three of you."

"Well, I hate him," I said emphatically.

"Don't say that, Damiana. He will always be your father and you have to love him very much. Both of you must love him."

Tamara was the first to nod. I snuggled up against Mother so she would think I also agreed with her.

Eduardo's little handprint didn't come out completely, but Father said nothing. He ordered the counterpane thrown out, just like that. *That's how you treat anything that ceases to serve your purpose, right?* The next day he filled the house with flowers for Mother. The only other time I saw so many flowers was during her funeral. Because her left cheek and lips were swollen, Mother had to stay at home for several days: she could not attend a reception at the Dutch embassy or a dinner with the minister. So on those nights, the three of us crawled into bed with her, revelling in having her to ourselves. The early evening silence gradually filled with the song of the cicadas, which lulled us with their rhythmic chitter. Mother's fingers slid through our hair as she made soothing promises she would never be able to fulfill.

Elena knows of my aversion to flowers. That is why, when she saw a young woman coming toward me with an enormous bouquet as we walked toward the dressing room, she blocked her path. "She is allergic," Elena said, with the gentlest of smiles, and asked her to take them away. Allergic is a good word – the perfect excuse that doesn't allow for questions or insistence.

When I walked into the room and saw Tamara, I wished I was allergic to everything around me so I would have a good excuse to flee. I felt almost guilty for enjoying the second act so much. The applause was still loud enough to reach us, and I regretted that Juan José had asked that we leave our bows to the end. Surely the audience was confused. Tamara had tried to erase the smell she had created by opening the window and burning a stick of incense. The noise from the cars was unbearable and the sandalwood was dizzying, so I extinguished the column of smoke under the tap and closed the window immediately.

"Surely you must think that I am missing my bohemian days . . ."

"That's something Eduardo would think, not me, Tamara," I answered automatically as I made ready to change.

Faustina came in quickly, grimacing at the pungent odour.

"Are you becoming a hippie, Damiana?" Realizing that her joke had not been to my liking, she moved to put away the dress I had been wearing.

"How long since you've seen Eduardo, Damiana?"

Tamara's question brought me up short. I had almost stopped counting the years since I had left for Paris and Eduardo had gone to Chicago to study. Tamara had stayed with Father, living for a while in Mexico, and then coming and going between Mexico City and the embassies of Buenos Aires and Lima. Those, I never visited. They moved back to Mexico City permanently when Father was offered an important job at the Ministry of Foreign Affairs. Tamara loved the elegance of the official gatherings and happily accompanied him to the cocktail parties and dinners and receptions. She was interested in meeting important people, and made a point of introducing herself as "the daughter of the ambassador." She thought that this might be the way to find her longed-for connection to television and theatrical fame, but it just never happened. Still, Tamara – who, as a child, had confronted him and later stolen his liquor – now allowed Eusebio Guerra to lead her by the hand when he escorted her, his chosen companion; she became a trained falcon, obeying his every order without resistance.

By contrast, I loathed diplomatic reunions, especially once I started studying seriously and began to win scholarships. From then on, Father – who in the past had always criticized my singing and my love of music – would ask me to sing for his guests. Tamara would beg him to let her participate, too, by offering to interpret a monologue in front of some backdrop which she would have secretly prepared ahead of time, and eventually he would agree. To my surprise, she always received greater applause than I did. While I vocalized daily and studied musical notation for several hours, learning songs and arias with an almost unhealthy discipline, I never saw or heard her practicing her monologues. She had an uncanny knack for memorization, and she moved her body with an enviable naturalness and appropriateness. Almost by instinct, she modulated her voice and gave the right intonation to her phrases.. Because Father wouldn't let her study formally yet, she used to buy books on what interested her, and read them with speed. She did not seem to need more.

Tamara mocked the amount of time I spent on my studies. "You're doing it all wrong! This is how you do it," and with that dismissal, she would hum the complete aria which I had just set out to learn. It drove me mad. We spoke less and less, and when we returned to Mexico City she finally convinced Father to let her study theatre, even if it was just for fun. Once she had secured his permission, she softened her sisterly competitiveness.

The night that we got drunk together would have been the best of times had it not been for Eduardo. Just how long had it been since Eduardo and I had seen each other?

I couldn't answer Tamara because Guido entered the dressing room. He greeted us with a deep nod and said to me quietly, "*Brava*, Damiana, that was sensational. But – please forgive me the intrusion – what has happened to your father that has everyone so worried?"

I had to take a breath before answering.

"He is in intensive care with grave respiratory failure. That is all we know," I replied.

As I heard myself uttering these words, dark clouds threatened my mood again. What is not said can be hidden away – it almost ceases to exist. But to give voice to my father's state was to bring it back into present reality, to start the pain anew. Guido caught my change in mood. Saying nothing else, he embraced me and then departed the room.

There were people outside. Surely they wanted to know what I had said. I was relieved that the encounter with Guido had been brief. Had it been longer, it would have fractured my determination to stay strong.

"Have you called the hospital, Tamara?" I dared to ask.

"No, I'm too afraid."

"Is Eduardo coming?"

"Yes, his flight is on the way. He will meet us in the hospital," she said. "He's coming with Samantha."

That's how I learned that he was still with the same girl. Slim, with pointed features and an incisive sense of humour, Samantha always had an unpleasant comment up her sleeve, a gratuitous checkmate that no one had provoked or expected. With us, she was the exact opposite of Mother. But she was different with Eduardo: attentive, sometimes even affectionate. I remembered her as one of those wild animals that seem so sweet in their dens but that never cease to be dangerous. I did not feel like seeing her. But did I want to see Eduardo?

The last time he and I spoke, I had just finished packing for my move to Paris. After so many moves, I was used to pulling up roots and not getting attached to belongings. All the same, I did not want to get rid of certain items that wouldn't fit in my luggage. I didn't want to leave them in Father's hands, because I didn't know where he and Tamara would be transferred next, or whether these objects would be safe. Eduardo had just dropped off Samantha at his house. He came in and sat next to me, looking impassively at the room's bare walls and the neatly arranged suitcases and boxes. The only things I was taking with me were my clothes and my music scores, I told him. I didn't know what to do with the rest. Eduardo said he'd take care of everything and promised that nothing would get lost. My flight left at dawn – before anyone else would be up – so I made my goodbyes that night. We embraced, and then he left my room with one of my boxes in his arms. I tried to detect some sign of emotion in his face but he avoided my eyes. I couldn't tell if he was sad that I was leaving. But a few months later, before he went to Chicago to study, he sent me my belongings along with a little note that was almost affectionate. He had taken good care of my things. (In the box, I even discovered a bag of potpourri. I knew that this had been Samantha's idea: like any good beast, she had a fine sense of smell.) She and Eduardo went to Chicago; Tamara and Father to Buenos Aires and then Lima. I settled into my small Parisian flat. The pieces of our family jigsaw puzzle had been apart ever since then.

Before the call came for the final act, Elena entered my room. Noting that I was calm, she came toward me with a smile and said, "Do you know what happened while we were singing?"

I shook my head. Faustina and Tamara looked at her expectantly.

"Some of the musicians took their TVs to the pit. Pretty normal, right? They had them on the whole time, quietly as usual. But suddenly there was a goal and they all jumped up at the same time as the stagehands up above. It seems that between them they made quite a racket. Did you hear anything?"

"No, and you?"

"No, but Guido is quite upset. Did he say anything to you?"

"No."

"Well, the poor guy is frustrated because he doesn't have anyone to complain to except us. The director of the Institute of Fine Arts doesn't want to reprimand the musicians or the technicians: we all know that if he did, the union would be sure to organize a public protest against him and demand he be removed from his position. And you have seen that this Marisita makes their lives difficult for any stupid thing, especially now that she is going deaf but doesn't want to accept it. And on top of all that, did you know that Guido found out this morning that the timpanist – the one who asked for a replacement for tonight for professional superstitions – is actually going to Acapulco with his buddies? Guido says that the same thing happened to him when they did *Tristan and Isolde* and that it had been worse in *La Traviata* because . . . ."

I stopped listening. One knows that these things happen even in the best of theatres and to the greatest of artists. In my interview with Marilú, I had just written about the famous anecdote of Monserrat Caballé. I wanted to tell Elena but there was no interrupting her, so I just concentrated on my costume. The cuff of my dress for the last act was badly folded, so I creased it carefully. I then poured myself a glass of water and drank it slowly. Ever since we were students together at the conservatory, Elena had been like that: very talkative and extroverted. The role of Cherubino suited her perfectly – not just because of her voice and slim frame but also because of her personality.

The third act began soon after, and Susanna's secret meeting in the garden with the Count was agreed. He thinks he's finally going to seduce my character – he doesn't know the one meeting with him will be his wife, the Countess, wearing my dress. The change of costumes meant Michaela now shared the colour purple with me. It was a trifling observation, but it lifted my spirits. My favourite part of the opera comes two scenes later when Figaro discovers that he is the son of Bartolo and Marcellina, the woman who wanted to marry him in order to collect the debt that he owed. *"Ecco tua madre!"* always makes me laugh. It is such fun to pretend that I don't know anything, to make a big jealous scene for Figaro and to slap him – "*Senti questa!*" – and then to find out the truth.

Through these scenes, Dimitri made me forget about everything once again, but when we returned to the dressing rooms I remembered something that Tamara had once said to me. She'd said that the scene where Figaro discovers Marcellina is his mother was "the great-grandmother of modern soap operas." I really scolded her. It seemed a sacrilege to compare Mozart and Beaumarchais with any television production, and soap operas especially were always badly acted and poorly written. Tamara did not reply, but I could tell that she felt diminished. When had Tamara ended, the one who would defend her under-appreciated talents so fiercely? Her face had started changing since then, and I only bothered to see the most obvious brush strokes. Maybe, if I had paid more attention, things would have worked out differently.

CRED

Tamara looks in the mirror and doesn't know which way to comb her long hair. She considers that, in truth, neither side is her better one and that the best choice would be to forever turn into a woolly dog. The television studios faced the same problem. Even when the stylists put her hair in curlers and fixed it with spray, it would gradually puff and curl and fly in all directions. It was as if her hair had a life of its own and did not want to obey anyone. She had thought it would be easier to find refuge in the theatre where, it was said, physical perfection was not necessary to access leading roles. Tamara remembers that for a while she was able to repeat her adolescent triumphs – those performances she gave for her father's friends to great applause. The precise movements and the melodious and convincing voice flowed with ease. But little by little, the acting became more difficult. It became harder to remember words and gestures. It was hard to remember even the day of the week. Landing a role became equally difficult.

She had fought so hard to stay in Mexico – to think purely of Mexico – only to find that what had given her peace had finally betrayed her, had turned her into a creature like the stray dogs that roam the city. If there is something Tamara can't stand, it's stray dogs. She feels a desire to run and save them from the pain of their abandonment and helplessness. But she never dares do it because she knows in her heart that they are like her. *Like fucking Bambi.* So she looks away and pretends they don't exist. And just now, she pretends that all that has taken place doesn't matter, and that the most relevant thing in this moment is to decide which way to part her hair. Since she doesn't like either side, she gathers her hair into a bun at the back. To pass the time and erase her thoughts while she waits, she picks up Damiana's notebook. She has the pen in her hand but does not write. This time, she reads:

THE FUNNIEST THING THAT HAS HAPPENED TO YOU ONSTAGE

The funniest thing didn't happen to me. The funniest thing happened to Montserrat Caballé, and it is a well-known anecdote that is sometimes told as if it had occurred to someone else. But I write it the way I heard it for the first time. Imagine this: in a production of Norma, *the great Caballé begins her aria, "C-a-a-a-a-a-a-a-sta D-i-i-i-i-i-i-va," then suddenly she stops and signals to the conductor to halt the music. The audience murmurs; no one knows what's going on. All this in the middle of the production! Caballé raises her eyes. She seems to be waiting for something. Finally, she shrugs and asks the conductor to continue. The diva's voice begins anew, but the same thing happens: the hand gesture, the attentive gaze, the signal to restart. Once again, she stops. But this time, when she lifts her eyes, she addresses some unseen stagehand up in the heights. "Either we all listen to your soccer match on the radio or I sing my aria, but not both!"*

Tamara doesn't laugh. She leaves a message for her sister: *Instead, why don't you talk about the musicians who do whatever they please? That is more fun.*

WHY DID YOU CHOOSE TO LIVE IN PARIS?
Aside from the fact that it is the city where I completed my voice studies (and thus I know it well and feel comfortable

there), Paris is a very central place to live and manage my career. I often sing in Europe, and Paris is close to most places. Besides, an artist rarely lives in her home – most time is spent in planes and hotels. I do have an apartment in Paris, but I only live there for a few days a year when I am not travelling to sing.

Tamara finishes reading her sister's response and remains pensive. At last she uncovers her pen and writes another message: *Don't kid yourself. You didn't move to Paris for geographical convenience. Why don't you and I talk about why you went there?*

She leaves the pen and the notebook on the counter and goes to look for a telephone. She can't wait any longer. She has to call the hospital.

附

WHY DID YOU CHOOSE TO LIVE IN PARIS? *What should I answer?* I didn't want to tell Marilú that I dwell in an apartment of no significance whatsoever. That I don't care about Paris. To be uprooted is the formative characteristic of an ambassador's child. You live in a house that represents the country – a house that is officially yours but in which you hardly live. You have no time to make friends. You get used to being a foreigner, changing neighbours, classmates, landscapes, languages. Tamara had wanted to set herself up in Mexico to reclaim her "lost" identity, but her indefinite accent and her face – so much like Father's – were a burden to her. In one of his few letters, Eduardo told me that he had adapted well to Chicago because "in the U.S. it is almost compulsory to blur your identity in order to mix with people and be accepted." In Paris, I remain nowhere and everywhere at once, shuttling with my two suitcases from one theatre to the next. I shall never cease my pilgrimage.

At a rehearsal, Michaela had asked me what upcoming engagements I had scheduled after *Marriage*. I proudly answered what I also wrote down somewhere in Marilú's interview: that I was scheduled for *Traviata* in Berlin, six performances of *La Bohème* in Paris, then Munich, Vienna, another *Elixir* in Barcelona and, the following year, my debut in New York. Would I be able to handle my nerves – that rat churning in my entrails – before the start of my New York performance? It made me uneasy just to think of it. Michaela had already sung in New York and had also finished some performances in Berlin, so she told me about these experiences – with an arrogance that I hope I'll never have.

The young woman who played Barbarina came close to us. She's the one I was forced, as Susanna, to listen to as she looked for the Countess' brooch all over the stage, singing an impeccable, if somewhat flat, aria. She looked at us almost with admiration, wanting to participate in what we were saying. Michaela excused herself, saying she didn't want to risk her voice by talking more, but she caressed the girl's face. Not knowing what to say, I also took my leave. The girl stayed behind, looking at us with a certain distrust that I doubt Michaela had noticed. That is why I have enjoyed working with Dimitri from the first. He is not conceited. He isn't interested in having an impressive collection of expensive watches and doesn't pay for restaurant bills with false gestures of smug generosity. He is different. My Susanna could not have a better Figaro.

I had to force myself to go back to Marilú's question. *Why did I choose to live in Paris?* Better to say something standard, reasonably credible. I didn't want to remember how it all had truly come to be.

❧ 4 ❧

When I entered the dressing room to change into the Countess' costume so we could trick the Count, Tamara was again teary-eyed, leaning against the window ledge, her gaze lost in no particular direction. Although she didn't say anything, I immediately sensed that Father was worse. But we were about to finish the performance, and I could not let myself be distracted. I bit my lip to avoid asking what I already knew. The traffic flowed easily now, and the lights that illuminated the Correos Building gave it a certain majesty. The smell of incense had begun to dissipate. Faustina helped me change quickly, and I left the dressing room urgently, repressing the undercurrent of foreboding. *And what if you die before telling me the truth, Father?*

One more act. The last one.

In the end, the orchestra played out of tune. It seemed that the little bald critic had been handed a weapon he could use to skewer the entire performance – from my shaky start, to the noise from the orchestra and the stage-hands in the second act, to the false notes in the closing. The woodwinds were so obviously off that Guido's back curved in shock as if he had been struck. In that poignant movement I witnessed his powerlessness: for fear of union reprisals he would not be able to reprimand the musicians. "This way, the opera in Mexico will always remain third-rate," I had heard someone say several days ago, but I had thought it a bitter exaggeration. I felt for Guido who had to live with this all the time, so I redoubled my efforts. I was going to finish as the best Susanna possible. During the reconciliation with Figaro, I was greeted with an unfamiliar glow in Dimitri's eyes that held me fascinated.

The ovation at the end was overwhelming, especially for Michaela. It is true that she deserved such an enthusiastic response, but I couldn't help feeling awkward, castigating myself for the early mistakes I had made. Even so, the applause I received was generous. More than I had expected or perhaps deserved. The audience's reaction was a surprise for all of us, but especially for me. I bent my head with well-rehearsed grace, looked out deliberately at the seats – up and down, right to left – and gave thanks with my companions, all of us holding hands to acknowledge the orchestra. *Couldn't you have come to listen to me sometime and see all this, Father – this enormous wolf's mouth filled with people that smile?*

Before the curtain descended, Dimitri gathered me into an enormous embrace and kissed me full on the lips. *"Brava,"* he said, leaning in toward my neck. I was speechless. Had he been anyone else, I would have slapped him. Instead, almost imperceptibly, I realized I did not want to pull away. I enjoyed the sensation of his moist skin against mine – sweat trickling down his sideburns, the smell of his body after all that singing. I liked the cool mint of his breath. So unlike that Turkish tenor I had partnered with in Italy, whose opened mouth reeked of kebabs with onions. Or the other one, who, embarrassed about sweating excessively under the lights, would drown himself in a bottle of cologne before each performance. He continued to douse himself between scenes, so that even with several metres of distance between us, his mere presence was enough to make me dizzy.

When the curtain finally closed, Dimitri held me briefly again before walking me to my dressing room. He asked if he could come to the hospital with Tamara and me. Elena, Faustina, and even Michaela also offered to come, but I said no to them all. Guido had organized a small celebration at his apartment, and I didn't want it ruined. Besides, what I really wanted to do was to get out of the theatre and stop giving explanations. I took longer than usual to undress because Juan José also came to hug me, as did even the technician with the perfect Italian. Someone brought me another flower bouquet that Elena took straight away to her dressing room. I had been wishing for the performance to be over so that I could go to the hospital right away, but this stampede was so gracious that, deep inside, I almost didn't want it to end, much less leave immediately as Tamara wanted.

Faustina offered to take care of my makeup, my scores, and my property, so that Tamara and I could exit quickly. We were both nervous, more than before. Someone on staff gave an excuse on my behalf to the members of the audience who wanted to greet me. And finally we were able to set off. I had completely forgotten about the notebook, so when Elena came by to retrieve it for Marilú, I could not say where it was.

Tamara could, though: "She hasn't finished saying what is needed. We will take it with us." She sounded so convinced that I didn't dare contradict her.

Elena nodded, kissed me, and moved aside to let us pass.

We were almost at the door when Rodrigo, violin case in hand, blocked our path. "Can I come with you?" he asked.

Dimitri, who had joined us despite my protests – who had abandoned the public's flattering attention and even the joys of Guido's party – took me by the waist and looked at my sister and me. I didn't know what to say to Rodrigo. I left the decision to Tamara.

osⲃꙮ

When Tamara sees Rodrigo with his coat on, ready to go with them, she finds in his eyes that old warm clay she nestled in her hands, and she suddenly remembers that his second toe is longer than his big toe, something she had always found amusing. She accepts his company. But the silence in the car is so heavy that she almost regrets it.

A billboard announcing Oreo cookies suddenly claws at her memory. Those cookies always give her a stomach ache. Tamara does not forget they are the ones she was made to eat at the clinic. It smelled excessively of chlorine, and it was very cold. "You have to eat these cookies and drink this juice, come on," a young woman – who was certainly not a nurse – had said. The thick nectar was so perfumed that it made it more difficult to tolerate the cookies. Then the box with antibiotics and the saddest walk in her life. The body hollow, an emptiness impossible to repair. *Life continues in your absence. In your absence I will breathe, and the rain will fall, and you will be but a memory that floats to the sea.* Tamara also doesn't forget – though she tries – the moment in which the doctor deposited the contents of the metal basin into the toilet and pulled the chain. *Why did he have to do it there, next to me?* That was the first time she didn't protest out loud, although she was so weak and defeated that she didn't even notice. After that, silence and screams took turns until weariness won out. What Tamara hates most is Oreo cookies, but she suddenly also hates this car journey next to Rodrigo, on the way to another death.

What I hate the most is everything I did for you, what I stopped doing for you, and everything implied in living as "*us.*" Even so, she feels the desire to rest her head on Rodrigo's shoulder. She blames weariness and forces herself to be strong, to sit more upright, to seem indifferent. *But I know that you don't believe me.*

os80

WHAT IS YOUR FAVOURITE INSTRUMENT

My first instinct was to write *all of them except the tim-pani,* but instead I wrote:

> *My favourite instrument is the violin, although what I really listen to are concertos for flute and orchestra. Bach in particular.*

Ever since Father silenced my mother's flute forever, I have taken every opportunity to give it life anew, to give it presence, to let myself be lulled by it. The violin, on the other hand, makes me afraid. Its beauty, like all beauty, is not to be trusted.

⪼ 5 ⪻

It was hard for me to remain calm in the car. Seeing Rodrigo and Tamara together stirred an old anger, pain I had thought forgotten.

Soon after our first and only drunken binge together, Tamara convinced me to introduce her to Rodrigo. Elena and I had just graduated from the conservatory. Rodrigo and I had met at one of the student recitals. When I first heard him play, it seemed that the violin was an extension of his body. When it was nestled comfortably between his shoulder and cheek, allowing itself to be caressed by his long fingers, it was as if all of them – violin, bow, and Rodrigo himself – danced together to the sound and tempo of copulation between gods. Not surprisingly, Rodrigo was the only one who got a standing ovation. When Elena offered to introduce us, I couldn't hide my excitement. His long curls, gathered into a ponytail, hinted at rebellion. The callus that all violinists acquire on their necks was not a rough spot on his skin – it was more like the mark of a permanent kiss. We found so much in common with each other that we soon began to make mutual plans: applying for scholarships, conquering the grand theatres, sharing our lives.

Our first plan was to travel to Cuba to explore the prestigious musical pedagogy of the island. "Imagine the excellence of the Russians but with the Caribbean sun," he would tell me. With Father's words ringing in my ears – *Russians don't have a sense of humour* – I would feel guilty and change the subject. Rodrigo was interested in everything to do with stringed instruments. He explored violins avidly, with delicacy and reverence, as if they were sacred beings. I loved to watch him lose himself in wood and strings because that same dedication made me vibrate under his fingers as they passed this way and that over my skin.

The trip to Cuba was postponed because he was asked, for the first time, to be a soloist with the Philharmonic. He became engaged in such a frenzy of study that he had time for nothing else. He wanted to prepare a most difficult Paganini for an encore. I then accepted some recitals in various cities around the country – small theatres, opportunities that were not comparable to what Rodrigo had before him, but good enough to expand my own experience. Just as he asked, I let him be so that he could concentrate fully on preparing himself and, meanwhile, I dedicated myself to my voice. That kept me busy while the business of the scholarship worked itself out. Father had already told me that if I persisted in being a professional singer, he would not support me. He would pay for "serious university study" but not for an "aspiring, refined circus artist." I will never forget his words because they were the engine that propelled me to search for the alternatives that would later save me. In the car, on the way to the hospital, I decided that I would thank him for it when we arrived. *Father, you have no idea what good you did me without meaning to.*

What had changed so much about Rodrigo's appearance? His eyes? His way of moving? I didn't dare look toward him in order to examine him and search out the answer. Instead, I leaned against Dimitri's shoulder and lost myself in the past.

I had wanted to surprise Rodrigo by showing up at the concert hall where he was going to play the Paganini. I made him think that I was still on tour, that an additional date had been added that would keep me out of Mexico City. On the phone, he told me he would miss me. That he would play for me. Be thinking of me.

I secretly returned the day of his concert. Elena had just discovered a beauty parlour that she strongly recommended. I accepted her offer to make an appointment. Afterwards, I scarcely had time to drop off my luggage at Father's house before dashing to the theatre. It was not unusual that there was no one in the house except for the maids to see me rush off with a new hairstyle and fingernails coloured like hard candy.

It was a Friday evening, and the traffic to the concert hall was worse than it had been earlier when I had emerged from the airport. I was sure I wouldn't get to the concert on time. *If I arrive late for the first part, I will not be allowed into the hall. I won't be able to listen to him play!* The taxi crawled through the horn-blowing of the other cars. Street vendors took advantage of the delays, threading through cars to sell pop, peanuts, and potato chips. There is nothing worse for a singer than peanuts. They scrape the throat and leave behind an unbearable breath that lasts an eternity because they leave the teeth encrusted with a kind of paste that begins to decompose. Whenever I think of peanuts I feel disgust, and that night the taxi driver bought himself two bags, which he proceeded to wolf down during the tedious journey. Maybe that is why as soon as I saw the marquee in the distance, I decided to get out of the car and walk.

I dodged people and stalls selling juice and cheap toys until I reached the concert hall. There was no one left in the lobby. At the ticket counter I was told that the performance had begun five minutes before. I begged them to let me through and showed my ticket and seat number but to no avail. It occurred to me then to sneak in through the back door, go toward the dressing rooms, and listen to the concert from there. I knew the way because we had sometimes been allowed to practice in the rooms that the orchestra used.

My heart was beating fast as I got close to Rodrigo's dressing room. On the door, a sign read SOLOIST. I felt so proud of him. The music played beautifully. The Beethoven was almost perfect and the notes could be heard all through the halls behind the stage. *If he is starting like this, the encore is going to be over the top.* The door was ajar, and I recognized his violin case on the counter in the back of the room. I entered confidently, relieved to have made it, when I noticed the photographs glued to the mirror and pasted inside his case. Tamara. In profile. In a forest wearing a favourite blouse of mine I thought I had lost. With sudden clarity, I understood the absences, the excuses, why he didn't sound too disappointed when I told him I wouldn't be with him that evening. I was left breathless for a few seconds, viscerally winded. It felt as if fists were striking my stomach.

At last I ran out. I bounded toward the street – my vision a blur – biting my fingernails as if they were my enemies, stripping away little peels of nail polish. I retraced my earlier steps to the concert hall, but I didn't recognize any of the vendors or the stalls. Everything was hazy. After I had walked for some blocks, the pain overtook me and I sat on the curb and began to cry so inconsolably that strangers stopped and asked if I needed help. A woman in brown shoes crouched down and asked me to get up. She said I couldn't stay there. "A girl as pretty as you can't cry in this way. Please, get up. Nothing is worth such suffering." I remained rooted, staring down at the ground and chewing what was left of my fingernails. That is why I only remember her shoes. I didn't turn to look at her. I felt her caressing my hair. She continued to speak but I couldn't comprehend her words because I felt like I was drowning in a waterfall – choking, breathless, the taste of salt water. A man pulled over in his car and gave me a box of tissues. I couldn't even say "thank you." It was no use drying my face because of the storm raging in my eyes. I have no idea how much time passed before I gathered the strength to stand.

Before taking a taxi back to Father's house, I walked for what seemed an eternity. That was the old days, when it was still safe to walk in the city. I was not afraid of anything. My skin was numb and my eyes swollen from crying. When I got home, only Eduardo was there. I was so blinded when I went into Tamara's room that I only remember fragments of what happened: the clothes I tore, the photos I smashed, the furniture I wounded. Eduardo came in. He grabbed me from behind and held my arms. We struggled, but soon I was bent double from the blow that, hours earlier, had robbed me of air. I wept as my brother's chest pressed against my back. The strange thing is that he didn't ask anything – it was as if he'd guessed what had happened or had known it all along. Once I grew passive, he took me to my room and brought me a cup of chamomile tea that cooled long before I remembered to drink it.

I wondered what face Eduardo would make at the hospital when he saw Tamara, Rodrigo and me sitting calmly together. Perhaps I would get up the courage to ask him about that night – if he had known about Tamara and Rodrigo all along, and, if so, how had he found out and why hadn't he forewarned me.

At that moment, Tamara roughly cut into my train of thought. She scolded me for giving a coin to the little boy who leapt onto the hood of the car to clean the windshield but left it dirtier than it had been. "We must not give them even one peso. They use it to buy drugs," she emphasized, bothered. But I can never refuse these children, any person asking for help on the street. The street is the worst place in which to be alone. I never told anyone about my street-side weeping, and ever since that night I have always given what little help is asked: with coins, with directions, with anything. I do it because I know what it is like to feel like dying, to have nowhere to go, and to find people to whom, for a few seconds, you matter. *Father, you – like Tamara – will never understand this.*

ᏨᏋᎦ

Tamara thinks about her mother. She does not forgive her for dying. *You never really loved us.* She is sure that any woman who allows herself to be beaten deserves a worse punishment than the beating itself. Her dad had said, "Don't ever allow it. I didn't raise stupid daughters, and especially you who are the only one to know the complete truth." And then he kissed her, complicit, on the cheek.

That is why, when that film producer slapped her during an argument, she took the metal candelabra and smashed it over his head when he wasn't looking. *From behind and so you die, asshole.* But she became paralyzed with fear when she saw the blood flowing from the grey-haired skull. She called an ambulance, left the door ajar, and escaped before anyone arrived. She took the candelabra with her, feeling a strange mixture of fascination and disgust for the blood shining on it. It is with a bitter smile she recalls that this had been BR/BC. Before Rodrigo. Before the clinic.

Upon remembering the candelabra, two searing words fill her mind: Canopic jars. *I need four of them: one to keep my mother's blood, one to recover the blood swallowed with a roar by the pipes while I ate an Oreo, one to collect the blood of those who have harmed me, and a last one to safeguard my father's before he dies . . . and a carrying case to have them with me always. In order to remember that they exist, to smell and touch those lives that only breathe through my skin, even if they exist just because I remember them.*

CRBD

SOME SUPERSTITION YOU HAVE BEFORE GOING ON STAGE

After what had just happened with my wardrobe in this production, I thought it prudent not to go into detail about colours. And I was too lazy to talk about the bent nails that stagehands leave lying around so that those who believe them to be good luck take courage. Personally, I have never dared to write "Macbeth" inside a theatre, let alone say it out loud. There are those who will become quite upset – they consider it a terrible omen – and for me it is important to maintain a cordial relationship with my colleagues. So instead I wrote:

I like what we say to each other before we begin. The Germans say "Hals und Beinbruch." *That means "Break your neck and one leg." Generally, in most theatres, people say* "Merde," *or something of the sort, which means "A lot of shit." Someone told me that this began long ago when people travelled to the theatre by carriage, and horses would naturally defecate around the building. The more shit there was, the larger the audience, and the better the chance that the show would be a success. In the opera, we say* "In bocca al luppo" *and* "Creppi il luppo" *which are something like "Let's go to the wolf's mouth" or "Kill the wolf." In English, they say* "Break a leg," *which I find unoriginal. It's insipid but it works, I guess. Everything works as long as you don't wish for good luck. Good luck is very bad luck indeed.*

I didn't know if that entry made sense, but I decided not to cross it out. After all, I thought Marilú could always restructure it later.

❧ 6 ❧

The journey to the hospital was interminable. I remembered the last interview question I had managed to
answer before Tamara arrived. I remembered it, in particular, because I was in the midst of wishing for ready-made
phrases, magic words to conjure good fortune before
arriving at a hospital – just like the words we exchange
before going onstage. There ought to be something one
could say aside from "good luck" – some word that would
produce a good result, that meant that the difficulty
ahead would be brief, that gave courage. But I could not
find any that worked.

My head started to ache. I regretted allowing Rodrigo
and Dimitri to accompany us. I wondered what we would
have done if Guido hadn't insisted on sending us his car
and driver. Tamara and I were so distracted and exhausted
that neither of us could have managed. I asked her at what
time Eduardo's flight was arriving. "At one." Not long from
now. Dimitri's cough reminded me that he was still there,
that the shoulder I was leaning on was his. I had become
too distracted with my thoughts elsewhere. I turned to look
at him, and he smiled at me. *What is he doing here?* I asked

myself. What had been weaved between us in this singing wedding night was a mystery.

When we walked into the hospital, I was stung by the smell of disinfectant. Intensive care was on the second floor, in a freezing corner of the hospital. When I complained about the cold, I was told that because the equipment was in continuous use, it required cool temperatures to avoid overheating. Before entering Father's room, Tamara and I were asked to disinfect our hands and arms and don robes and masks. Rodrigo and Dimitri, clearly uneasy, remained outside. A nurse guided us to Father even though Tamara already knew the way. I was afraid to get close. I stayed a few paces back from the curtain that separated him from an old lady with opaque hair and blank eyes. Sounds assaulted me. The quiet, purposeful steps of the nurses, the constant drip of the IVs, the atonal beeping of the machines. A sudden alarm startled me. The medical team immediately mobilized to the corner opposite where I was standing. Two or three quick commands from a doctor, a rush of energy, and once again a calm punctuated with *beep beep beep*.

I had to think of something else to block out the noise, to avoid becoming depressed by what surrounded me. Something cheerful . . . *The amusement park*. When we were children, Father used to take us there, especially after Mother was no longer with us. In almost all the cities where we lived, there was at least one such park, and he had fun taking us out, watching us at the games as we took aim at the targets. Eduardo had a naturally accurate aim which Father coached him improve. Tamara was very good at playing with marbles. By contrast, I never won any prizes. While my siblings always emerged with trophies, I was perpetually empty-handed. It made me even angrier since I was the oldest – I was therefore supposed to be, and expected to be, the best. Father encouraged me, and I continued to make an effort. One day, I saw an enormous stuffed yellow duck that I was determined would not get away. I had three chances to win. My hands became sticky and moist. I failed on my first throw. My stomach started to ache. I missed the second one. Eduardo and Tamara began to taunt me, but Father told them to be quiet. On the third try, I clenched my teeth and threw as hard as I could . . . I failed once again.

I cried copious tears. I asked Father to win it for me, to buy it, but he refused. "One must win by fair means, Damiana," he told me. No matter how much I begged, he ignored me. I was angry for several days. That same week, I had an especially difficult exam, one that Father knew was important. The day after I got the results back and learned that I had done well, I came home to find the yellow duck sitting on my bed. When Father returned from the office, I ran to thank him. And I let myself be held in the arms of that immense man called Eusebio Guerra.

I didn't know if I wanted to see him now. I preferred to remember the image of that former Eusebio. The memory of the amusement park didn't soothe me. Instead, it exacerbated my desire to flee. I was about to follow my instinct when Tamara called. I couldn't leave now. I took a deep breath to give me courage, and I walked toward her.

It was terrifying – that shrunken, hapless man, his veins invaded by tubes, an enormous machine breathing through his mouth. I had to bite my fist through the mask to suppress a scream. *When did you turn into this, Father?* The skin greenish, thin, almost transparent. The black hair that Mother liked so much was now almost completely ghost-coloured. Dark circles had been carved under his eyes with a knife. I felt cheated and wanted to protest: this could not be my father. Tamara leaned down to kiss his forehead and whispered that I was there, too, that both of us were. "Lalito is on his way, Dad. But I'll leave you with Damiana. I'll be right back."

I imagined that Tamara was bidding Rodrigo goodbye. I didn't want to be there to witness it, but neither did I want to stay here looking at Father until she returned. The transformation was not credible. *Worse even than Gregor Samsa, Father. You have turned into a worm.* I backed away toward the old lady in the next bed and counted the beats of Father's breathing as if I were conducting a melody: one-two-three-four, out; one-two-three-four, in; one-two-three . . . Anything to avoid thinking about the dry saliva at the edges of his mouth, his skin like paper that had been crumpled and then smoothed. Doubts assailed me. *What had Mother really been like?* Maybe my memories of her also betrayed me and she was nothing like how I evoked her. Oh, to have her hand with me so I could calmly remember. How repulsive to think of staying now with Father's hand. Had we been elephants, I would never have known to lie down next to this little man to die. I would have rubbed all bones until I came across the strongest ones, convinced they were my father's. And in doing so, I would have died in the wrong place – but perhaps happy not knowing the truth. *But it is important to find out the truth. So then? If that's so, why don't you ask him again what you need him to tell you, before he's not able to anymore?*

I couldn't stand being in there with Father. I escaped to the waiting room and looked for Tamara but only found Dimitri. I let him wrap his arms around me, but his hold made me fearful. Father had been just like that, strong. *Just like that.* So I held Dimitri hard against me to burn the memory in, to engrave the sensation in the marrow of my bones. Tamara came in as Dimitri and I were saying goodbye, and so we two sisters, seated on a drab couch, waited for Eduardo.

The initial silence was frightening, as though we had chanced on a path of burning embers that we had to cross barefoot. Neither of us wanted to take the first step in conversation. I assumed that Rodrigo had left. We sipped our vending machine coffee without looking at each other.

Tamara looked very different that last time I saw her, the day after Rodrigo's concert. She arrived home at noon. Eduardo had already departed, and I was still wearing yesterday's clothes – dirty, my makeup smeared, my salon hairdo a wreck. When Tamara went into her room and saw the chaos which the maid had tried in vain to fix, she came looking for me. I was lying listlessly in bed, and it took me a few seconds to react. Then I leapt to my feet in front of her, and before she could say anything I spat in her face. She was not expecting it, but immediately she motioned to attack me. And in that split second, my arm took on an unfamiliar life of its own. I smashed my fist against her face with a force of which I had been completely unaware of having at my command. My fingers were still injured from the previous night – I had bitten my index finger till it was almost raw – but even with that, I split Tamara's lips open – the lips with which she had kissed Rodrigo. I was pleased for a brief moment. But then I was overwhelmed by the image of my mother with her bleeding mouth, by Eduardo's little handprint on the bedspread. Perhaps Tamara had also remembered this at the same moment because our sudden silence overflowed with a sadness that drenched the air.

I left two days later for Paris, choosing to await the results of the scholarship application from there. I lived on my savings, and crossed my fingers that I would be accepted at the conservatory so that I would never have to return to Father's house. I didn't say goodbye to Tamara, nor allow her to explain anything to me. I didn't want to hear a word from her or from Rodrigo, so it was months before I found out what had occurred at the concert.

It was Elena who told me, when she came to see me in Paris, that Rodrigo's debut had been a fiasco. He forgot a series of measures that left him paralyzed onstage, and though he tried to catch up with the orchestra, he could not. The conductor stopped the music and offered to start again but Rodrigo shook his head, excused himself and left the stage. Elena had heard nothing about him for some time until she was told that he had been hired for the opera's orchestra with a tenured position, forever hidden amongst the second violins.

"Do you like Paris?" Tamara asked me.

"Of course I like it. I love it."

There was an uncomfortable silence.

"What is one of your days like?" she asked.

"Calm. I get up early, go out for something to eat and return home to study. Sometimes I have rehearsals, and at night I go out with friends," I lied.

Of course Tamara noticed. She knew I had never been gregarious. "I can still tell when you are trying to deceive me."

"I have never been the one who lies," I said in my defence. I immediately felt ashamed of my outburst. I exhaled and tried to regain my composure.

"What I like best about Paris is a park a few blocks from my place. It is quite small and has only one bench which is usually empty. I go whenever I can, and I sit down to read. When it's very cold I settle for just the walk – I listen to the ice and snow crunching under my feet. But the best time is in April. There are birds and flowers and it smells of fresh grass. It's not warm, but the sun is out. That is the Paris I enjoy. The one that the tourists don't know exists. Where there isn't even one Japanese taking pictures. The Paris of my bench in the park."

Tamara sighed and nodded her head as if thanking me. We sat in silence for a few seconds until she took heart enough to speak again. "Can I ask you something else that has nothing to do with Paris?"

I sipped my coffee and shrugged.

"Have you forgiven me yet?" she asked.

I considered my answer for a moment. I was surprised by the directness of her question. "I don't know. I don't think so," I answered as honestly as possible.

Tamara placed her coffee on the table. "Will you let me tell you what happened? I would like you to know."

By way of reply I set my eyes on the cup resting in my hands and nodded. This had to happen one day. *Might as well be now.*

Tamara lowered her voice. "I had wanted to hook up with a producer, remember? But he didn't pay me any attention. Well, yes. He went to bed with me and then played dumb so as not to give me any important part in his soap opera. He thought I should settle with playing the protagonist's aunt, the standard one that appears in all soaps whenever the star needs a shoulder to cry on. I couldn't tolerate that. It also started to go badly for me in the theatre. I don't know why but I was finding it very hard to memorize my lines, and I began to forget my rehearsal times – I kept arriving late. I don't know what happened to me."

I knew what happened, and so did she. A lot of tequila is what happened.

"With Rodrigo, everything was different. He seemed so perfect that I couldn't stop thinking about the Silvio Rodriguez song – you know the one? – 'I am happy, I am a happy man, and I want on this day to be forgiven by the dead, for my happiness.'"

I was startled and had to stop her. "You'd better stop. I wasn't dead. And besides, I don't know that song."

"Silvio – the Cuban folk singer. Of course you know."

"The one that sings like a eunuch with a cold?"

She was offended, and I was pleased. Once again, she could not defend herself. I realized that my wish that she be unhappy, that even the most insignificant things turn out badly for her, had, in some way, come true. The only thing was that I could not be pleased about it. I was filled with unease, even remorse.

"If you don't let me finish telling you, you won't be able to understand." Her tone of voice had suddenly changed. It had become slower and deeper.

I examined her face, peered into her eyes.

"I got pregnant with Rodrigo's child, did you know?" she murmured, covering her face with the hair she had just let down.

I was speechless. She had been a falcon obedient to Father's wishes; what had happened? It couldn't have been an accident. My sister would never have been so naïve, so careless. Or would she? Was it then that Tamara the Fierce became lost and this stranger – who went through life like a small injured animal – arrived? I immediately assumed it was all Rodrigo's fault, and hated him doubly for it. I was about to ask Tamara not to tell me anything more; I didn't think it necessary.

But she spoke even more softly and signalled me to come closer. "We went to an underground clinic. We couldn't have that baby. Can you imagine the scandal Dad would have made? We had no savings or any kind of steady work. We arrived in the afternoon and the procedure took two whole hours. The worst thing was being semi-conscious and hearing everything. If you could have seen it . . . It was a private home where all the rooms smelled of chlorine and dampness. An hour after it was over, they released me with a prescription for antibiotics, and that was it. Just imagine what that place was like . . . . Afterwards, Rodrigo took me to his apartment. Do you remember his place?"

Of course I remembered. It was a two-bedroom apartment in a small co-op complex in the south of the city. It was a grey and white building without an elevator, but that didn't matter as he lived on the first floor.

Tamara continued talking as if afraid that with a pause she would not be able to continue. "Well, that very day he forgot his house keys. It was around seven or eight when we arrived. That very day he forgot the fucking keys to his apartment. He went to look for a locksmith but took God knows how long. Meanwhile, I was left there, sitting on the tile floor. Some neighbours asked me if I needed help, suggested I go to their home to wait for Rodrigo. They offered me water and food, but I was neither hungry nor thirsty and I didn't want to go to anyone's house. It was an eternity. A dangerous eternity, as it gave me time to think about all that had happened. How could I have allowed myself to be so irresponsible? And then, how could I have let the pregnancy get so far along? I didn't know what it was about Rodrigo that had changed me – made me stupid enough to betray everything I had been taught, everything I believed in. I still don't have an answer for that. Anyway, it became cold and my teeth began to chatter. I'm not sure whether it was from nerves, fear, the realization of what had just happened – or the combination of all these things and the cold tile floor I had been sitting on such a long time. But when Rodrigo arrived with the locksmith, I was unable to get up. The next day, he took me home and neither Dad nor Eduardo noticed anything. Rodrigo and I continued to see each other for a short while, but nothing was the same. One day, I couldn't stand it anymore and decided to stop seeing him. I stopped answering the phone. Dad had told me, you know? When you left he warned me that 'happiness is not built on someone else's pain.' More or less that's what he said. He already knew it wouldn't work, but he couldn't have imagined to what degree Rodrigo and I would fail. Why did we end up with such a bastard for a father?" Her eyes filled as she continued, "So adorable and such a bastard."

She stopped for a second and then looked me in the eye again. "I never thought that living with myself and the consequences of my actions would be so hard. I didn't know the implications of doing so many things badly. If it is of any use to you, I swear that I had not seen Rodrigo since then. Really. Until tonight, we have not seen each other at all. And if Dad hadn't become ill I wouldn't have gone to the theatre to look for you. Forgive me."

Her eyes were broken in a thousand pieces, joined by tiny red veins. I put my arm on her shoulders and she leaned toward me like a puppy, without another word. That is how Eduardo and Samantha found us.

~ 7 ~

A few weeks before I discovered the affair between Rodrigo
and Tamara, I had a conversation with Father that had been
so difficult that I didn't know what I would say to him if he
did regain consciousness. Would I be strong enough to
insist on the same point? Should I bother? I still remember
the time. It was nine-thirty in the evening. It was the time
when Father came out of his study and went to his bedroom. I was standing by the door when he emerged and I
asked him to stay with me so we could talk. There was
something I needed to ask him, something I couldn't wait
another minute to find out.

"Did you have Mother killed?"

His eyes revealed genuine surprise. The messy, bushy
eyebrows frowned, showing him ill at ease. For a moment I
thought he would rage like before, and that this time he
would really strike me. But then he went back into his
study and sat down.

"What kind of question is that?" he said in a quiet voice
which revealed either fury or sadness, I couldn't tell which.

"One that I have wanted to ask for a long time but
haven't dared."

He shook his head, incredulous.

"Tell me the truth. I need to know. Please," I insisted.

He made an effort to remain calm and to answer me with equanimity. "Why do you think that?"

"Because I heard you threaten her. The day that we returned from watching *Carmen*. You told her you were going to kill her. I remember clearly. Tamara and Eduardo heard also, but I don't know if they remember as well as I do. I hope not. I have never dared to ask them. Father, listen. There are nights when I can't sleep thinking of the beatings you gave Mother, and I'm tired of not being able to talk about her." Words were failing me. "I'm tired of not being able to speak of things straightforwardly and by their name. That is why I want to know if you had her killed."

Father stood up quickly and looked me in the eye. "You, who came with me to the burial, who saw me that day and all the others, you who noticed everything, how can you think this?" He changed his tone and looked downwards. "Leave this room. I don't want to see you."

Since I didn't obey him, he chose to leave himself, and so I was left without an answer. From that day on, Father avoided me as much as possible. He left for work quite early and came home when he knew I was out. When our eyes met by mistake in some room or hallway, I found it impossible to read his expression. I couldn't tell if he was genuinely hurt or trying to deceive me. I didn't know if Father ran from me because he felt betrayed or because he felt guilty. I left for Paris unable to say goodbye because he wasn't around when I discovered Rodrigo and Tamara. I thought of leaving a small note on his desk but, when I tried to write, I found nothing to say to him. I was about to throw my stuffed yellow duck into the garbage, but I left it on what used to be my bed so that Father wouldn't forget that we had business pending. I wanted to tear up the family photo I always have with me – but I lacked the courage.

☙❧

"What's wrong with him, Doctor?"

The neurologist adjusted his glasses on his nose and looked at the four of us: Eduardo, Samantha, Tamara and me. He paused. He seemed to be searching for the precise words with which to answer my brother's question.

"We are discarding different possibilities. It is not an embolism because the problem lies on both sides of his body, not just one. Most likely we are dealing with a neurological problem of viral origin, which we are investigating."

"Is he going to live?" Tamara asked.

"It depends. If it's the syndrome we suspect, there is a ninety percent chance of complete recovery through rehabilitating exercises. It would take a period of two years. But in the case of paralysis of the respiratory muscles, the diagnosis becomes complicated."

"What is the percentage?" Samantha wanted to know.

"The statistics show that five percent die quickly because they are unable to breathe again on their own."

Eduardo appreciated the sincerity of the doctor. I was thankful that no one asked if Father was in that five percent.

My brother's voice sounded very much like Father's. I saw him changed as well. He had grown a moustache that made him look older and had gained several kilos which he attributed, half smiling, "to the good life in Gringoland." Samantha was as slim as always, with longer hair and hardened features. I was expecting her to complain about the hospital smell if nothing else, but she did not. She stayed at Eduardo's side, holding his hand the entire time. The four of us stood at the foot of Father's bed for a while, but only Tamara chose to speak.

"You see, Dad, we are all together – just like you wanted. You have to get better."

Back in the waiting room, Tamara suggested that I pull out the family photo from my bag so we could all look at it together. Guido's driver had left my things with the nurses' station – the nurses had agreed to hold on to my belongings while Tamara and I went in to see Father. Eduardo seemed enthusiastic about Tamara's idea and so did Samantha, even though she didn't know what photo we were talking about.

While they looked at the picture, I thought about that fateful day and, in my mind, went over the details I remembered.

"Look, Mom, a cartwheel!" Tamara shouted, and Mother turned to watch her. In that white suit she seemed to come out of a canvas, the eyes blue and the hair shiny like a Renaissance Madonna. Mother applauded Tamara's cartwheel.

Eduardo, dressed as a policeman, was chasing Father about the garden. His little, high-pitched voice was authoritarian even then: "Stop! You are under arrest!" and Father surrendered his thick wrists so Eduardo could try to shackle him with his toys of justice.

I was sitting on the swing, fighting with my dress which kept billowing in the air, threatening to reveal my underwear. Tamara came up to me with a long-legged spider between her fingers.

"Mom!!! Dad!!! Tamara wants to throw a spider at me!!!"

"You are such a tattletale, Damiana."

Mother sat on the grass and Dad set up a chair next to her. It was hot, but a salt-laden breeze kept us cool. There was the sweet aroma of fruit. The voices of Eduardo and Tamara chasing each other in the garden could be heard loud and clear. I saw Mother pluck a flower with her toes and offer it to Father. They kissed. I think it's the only time that we saw them kissing, so we

began to tease them. "Eeeeeew, kiss, gross, slobber . . . ."
They laughed.

Father was happy for some reason I can't remember, and that day we all went for an early breakfast at a nice restaurant.

Upon returning home, we raced back to the garden to play. Mother laughed at the witty remarks of Eduardo the policeman, and asked Tamara to get down from the tree: "You're like a monkey, it's dangerous." Father said, "Just let her be. She is brave, she's a good climber," and, "Look at her, no one will ever stop her," and me on the swing, pretending to fly.

Just then, Mother went into the house. She came back with the butler and the camera in hand. It was a new model, the instant kind – large and heavy, with a long flash that was purchased separately and that clicked onto the top of the camera. She had decided to use it for the first time, and so we huddled together: Tamara wearing her deep red pants, Mother in her bright white suit, Eduardo with his policeman's cap (firmly placed with Father's help), Father with a shirt as yellow as the amusement park's duck – a yellow I didn't yet know and couldn't have imagined – and me in my favourite dress. We took four pictures; one for each of us children, and one for Mother. But at the hospital I learned that neither of my siblings had kept theirs. They wanted to make copies of mine and were happy that it still existed.

It had survived because I first kept it in a book, then in my musical scores, and finally in my carrying case. Maybe I should have whispered that to Father when I saw him in the hospital bed, to see if he remembered that day, to see if he'd react in some way. Tamara insisted on showing him the photo even though he couldn't open his eyes. She was sure about the benefit of letting Father know that we were all together once again. Eduardo obeyed and leaned over to mutter something I could not hear, and she shook her head. Samantha remained, as always, at Eduardo's side, indifferent to us but attentive and loyal to him.

I would have liked to ask Father what he imagined would hurt more: dying from a bullet wound like Mother or drowning slowly in mucous like him. I wondered if Tamara or Eduardo ever asked about the truth of what had happened. Or if they tried to find out of their own accord. I did, but never told them. After I moved to Paris, I obtained the news report regarding Mother's death. I received a copy from the Caracas' newspaper archives after enduring weeks of bureaucratic delay and annoying red tape.

The paper said it had been a mugging. Caracas was a dangerous city even then. One could not take a cab, and the windows and doors of every house, apartment building, and business were protected with one or two rows of metal bars. People said – I could remember clearly – that it was wise to carry a few *bolívares* in one's wallet in case of mugging, so as to not enrage assailants. During casual chats, we found that robberies occurred in apartment elevators, in parking lots . . . "Venezuelans are tough," Father used to say, "not like us Mexicans who just give in." (I would have liked to ask his opinion about our country now that it seems like a branch of that Caracas from twenty years ago . . . .) They never caught the culprits. They remain free, those tough Venezuelans, who shot my mother so they could steal her watch. She was driving down an avenue, and they accosted her at a red light. That is what a witness said. Something happened and they fired. They only took her watch. That watch cost an accurate bullet to the head. The press made a scandal, which I only discovered when I set out to find the truth for myself. Father had protected us well. It was a good thing he got us out of the country almost immediately.

That is why I don't wear a watch. That is why I get furious when my friends boast about the prices of theirs. That is why I like Dimitri, who doesn't wear a watch either. He agrees that it is better to ask other people the time.

"What time is it?" I asked.

"Four in the morning," Samantha, nodding off, complained. Eduardo offered to take her to the hotel.

"Hotel?" I asked.

"Yes, it's more comfortable than staying at Father's house," he explained.

I understood what he meant. Father's house was no longer our house. It was his and Tamara's only. I was also staying in a hotel.

Had Tamara and Eduardo ever thought that Father had something to do with Mother's death? I was desperate for him to live so that he could answer me. But I didn't dare ask my siblings, or voice my words to Father's shrunken body at this moment.

ΣβΩ

Tamara cannot believe that Rodrigo has come back to the hospital looking for her, and when she goes outside to speak with him, to ask him to leave, she can't believe what she hears.

"I have missed you so much. I still need you."

The emptiness in her belly contracts. Tamara has left her sister with their father. She hasn't yet been able to explain anything to Damiana. *How dare you, Rodrigo?* She controls herself to keep from screaming, but when she opens her mouth, searching for words, her voice does not come out, it's stuck between her throat and teeth. She needs to protest against Rodrigo. *For your lack of balls in confronting Damiana when you decided to stay with me, and for not defending our relationship before my father, and for letting me go alone into that horrendous room where you didn't see or hear what was done to me, and for not defending your violin the day of your ruined concert. You are a cowardly piece of shit!* But she can say nothing. She cries. The sound of the passing cars shelters her weeping. She senses that no one but he can hear her, and that it is possible to let herself go. Rodrigo hugs her and she beats his chest, but soon she collapses and holds him as well. She notices that it's true. *Skin has a memory*, and the smell of Rodrigo makes her feel safe. *The cowardly piece of shit is me for not wanting to let you go.*

Cৰেৰ

Dawn has always made me sad. After the comfort that night-time offers, the first rays of light fall like knives on the eyes. That early morning in the hospital was particularly aggressive. Samantha had taken a taxi to her hotel. Tamara, Eduardo and I sat quietly next to each other in the little waiting room, drinking coffee, and we saw how the sun came up through the windows, making nothing look better.

Dimitri arrived early with some pastries and freshly squeezed juice. I looked at him in surprise: the previous night had been different. We had been Susanna and Figaro – we had sung against adversity and triumphed. But what did he think, turning up here at the hospital, to bring us breakfast? What would I do when I had to return to Paris, travel to all those other cities and carry on with my engagements? Romance is not practical when one is a singer. It gets in the way. It steals time from studying. It distracts. I was going to tell him this, but he was so affectionate and effusive that I didn't have a chance. He introduced himself to Eduardo with amazing ease and sat next to us to keep us company. *You would like him, Father, even though he is Russian.*

Dimitri insisted, but I couldn't eat. We barely touched the pastries. The only thing I finished was the juice. Too many coffees had made me thirsty.

Tamara took advantage of that moment to excuse herself so she could go home to rest and shower. She seemed calm. Samantha arrived a little later. Eduardo, she, Dimitri and I were left. I didn't know how to begin explaining why Figaro was there with me.

Eduardo and Samantha went in to see Father, and when they came out Eduardo asked me if I wanted to go in as well. "He looks better than yesterday," he said by way of encouragement. Dimitri backed him up. He thought it was a good idea for me to see my father, to speak to him. I couldn't stand the pressure I felt from them – all three of them – after all, Samantha's silence could only mean she was preparing herself to strike. I didn't want to wait for that to happen. That's the only reason I obeyed.

His eyes were closed as if in sleep.

"Are you awake, Father?"

I got close to his ear and stroked his forehead, trying to recognize it.

"I need to ask you many things, and I need you to answer me. Are you listening?"

Silence. *Beep, beep, beep.* Air going into Father's chest, thanks to the respirator. Nothing else. It didn't matter. I would continue, speak of something else first. Perhaps that would work better.

"In the waiting room, there is a singer who thinks he is my boyfriend. He is Russian. Can you believe it? Just like Mother. But he is very cheerful and actually has a sense of humour. You know how he found out that he wanted to sing? He was given a record of arias, an LP. And he liked it so much that he saved his money to buy a recording of a complete opera. He lived in Moscow and was very poor, like you were when you were young. Remember when you told us that you ate peas every day because you couldn't afford anything else? Well, he was the same. Just like Mom, too, and like all the other 'starving Soviets,' as you used called them. His mother was a seamstress. She made theatrical costumes – some of them for the ballerinas of the Bolshoi. Isn't that an almost poetic job? He was twenty-two when he began to study singing. Before that, he had been a mechanic. I can't imagine that. When you meet him, you won't be able to imagine it either. He told me all this one day in a dressing room, the first time we sang together."

I stopped to see if there was any reaction. Nothing. So I went on.

"But he kept studying, and as soon as he could, he left Moscow and continued his lessons in England. He is very tall; I might even call him handsome."

I stopped intentionally, again waiting for something to happen.

"And last night he sang *Figaro* with me. Did you find out that I was going to have my debut here, Father? Or did you not care? Tamara said nothing. Would you have come to see me if you hadn't fallen sick? You used to be proud of me, even if you deny it. That's why you used to show me off to your guests when I let you."

I waited. I watched him carefully to see if I could detect any movement in his eyes or fingers.

"Your fingernails are bluish. Are you cold?"

I found a blanket to better cover him up, and I wrapped it around him, careful not to move the needles and tubes attached to his hands and feet.

"I have been thinking a lot about Caracas, Father. Remember?"

I stammered, about to run out of there. Instead, I got close to him, looked him in the face, and insisted: "Are you going to die without telling me the truth?"

I closed my fists because of my helplessness and I tightened my lips so as not to scream from hopelessness. No reaction. I got closer and moved him a bit. His body was warmer and the beeps and other sounds from the machines indicated that everything was in order. My hands, my legs, my voice were trembling and I couldn't think clearly, but if I faltered I would lose my last opportunity to find the answer I so needed.

"What do you smell of, Father?" I got closer in order to smell him. "Of nothing. You, who always loved fine colognes. I still remember your favourite one. Would you like me to order you some? Whenever I see it in an airport shop I think of you, you know?"

And in spite of myself, I smiled, because I had never confessed that to anyone.

"Perhaps if we put some on you, it will give you new life."

There was still no reply. The movements I was aware of were from my own body, all stirred up.

"You can't die because you still need to hear me sing – in a professional theatre with a real audience, not just your guests. I have felt awful knowing you didn't look for me even once in all these years I've been away. You didn't even look me up when you went to Paris. Did you think I wouldn't find out you were there?"

I waited for a sign, counted six beeps.

"I am still upset, and that is not going to go away just because you are sick. You let me go without fighting. I appreciate it, but I don't forgive it. I need to feel that you loved me, the way I love you – Daddy – even if we never did say it . . ."

I felt as if I was going to fall apart so I changed my tone to appear more optimistic.

"You have to get better so we can talk about a lot of things. The three of us are here. Well, the four of us, because

Eduardo is here with Samantha. Tamara went off to take a shower but will be back later. My friend Elena promised to come as well. Remember her – the one you said talked like a quack? Last night we both appeared in *Figaro*. She played Cherubino, the young page. And you would have been proud of me," I lied, "because everything turned out great – in spite of you being here and me finding out only a few moments before I went onstage."

I began to feel stupid, talking to myself, discovering parts of my body I was unaware of because they had never before trembled. When she left, Tamara had been sure that Father heard everything, that he had been encouraged by hearing about the photograph and other memories.

"The thing is, I love you very much, but I cannot forget Mother. I loved her too, and I needed her so much." My tears began to flow silently. I found it hard to articulate the words. I had to lower my voice even more in order to make myself intelligible.

"Why did you let her go out alone the day they killed her? Where was your driver? He always went with us everywhere. Why didn't he go with her that day?"

I counted eight beeps as I waited for his reply – nothing. Counting the beeps was the only thing keeping me whole, coherent.

"Did you ever wonder if she suspected that the mugger wasn't a mugger, that he was an assassin you had sent? Or have I just been imagining it?"

I could feel someone coming near, but I didn't want to turn to see who it was.

"Tell me the truth. Did she really die over a fucking watch?"

And then my voice broke.

The nurse had to help me get to my feet. Before I left, I wanted to kiss Father on the forehead and promise him that, soon, everything would be the way it used to be. *No, much better than before.* But I couldn't. I remembered Mother. I decided not to promise anything I wasn't sure I could carry out.

The beeps marked my steps to the doorway. I was shaking and crying so much that one of the doctors offered me a tranquilizer, but I refused. The old lady from the previous day was no longer there. I didn't want to ask if she had died. The nurse walked me to the waiting room where Dimitri was expecting me. I hid my face in his chest. Not even the strength of his arms could still my shaking.

ᗰ�

Tamara had not gone home to take a shower. We found that out because Rodrigo had been looking for her. He reported that she wasn't at home and nobody had seen her.

"And just who does that guy think he is, exactly? What's he doing here?" Eduardo, his voice down, asked me when he saw Rodrigo coming.

"Tamara told him he could come."

The expression of disapproval in Eduardo's face coincided with mine, but the urgent thing was to find our sister. Eduardo decided to search for her near the hospital, and he asked that Rodrigo go to her favourite places, if he still knew what they were. Samantha stayed with Dimitri and me. She paced up and down the waiting room.

The doctor emerged, and as I was the only immediate relative he gave me the updates regarding Father's condition. I found it all hard to understand because I was exhausted – my head was throbbing and my pulse remained unstable. Then I remembered Marilú's notebook. I decided to use it to write down what the doctor was saying, so that Eduardo and Tamara could read it when they arrived. He mentioned a syndrome.

"What? Can you spell it for me?"

"G-u-i-l-l-a-i-n. Capital B-a-r-r-é."

Guillain Barré: This syndrome affects the body's peripheral nerves. It can cause weakness or paralysis. It is impossible to predict, and can manifest itself at any time. It has a viral origin, and it is necessary to perform more tests to definitely determine if it is what afflicts Mr. Guerra.

I had to reread the explanation several times to better understand it. I felt like everything around me was moving with a particular slowness, as if it were occurring in the distance, far away from me.

Eduardo took more than three hours to return. There was a clock on the wall and Dimitri kept track of time. During that whole period Samantha never sat down. She walked up and down the aisle as if she were unable to relax in my brother's absence. But, as soon as he arrived, she regained her composure and became her usual falcon self. Eduardo came in with a disturbed expression. It was he, not Rodrigo, who found Tamara in a cantina near the hospital. Our brother had taken her home, where he made sure she took a shower and ate something before going to sleep.

I told him that the doctor had made a preliminary diagnosis, and without thinking twice I handed him the notebook. I didn't think about everything else that was written in it – I just passed it to him. Dimitri suggested then that I, too, try to rest. But only if Eduardo kept watch at the hospital could I go back to the hotel in peace. "You don't mind, Lalito? You didn't sleep all night, either." He shook his head, gave me a peck on the cheek and went to sit next to Samantha.

Dimitri took me to the hotel to rest. We had a performance coming up on Saturday, and I couldn't afford to damage my voice. When we arrived at reception, I was given a message from the Institute's director (I never remember their names because they never keep their jobs for too long), offering to find me a replacement for Saturday night. "That is very generous, but there's no need," I told him on the phone before I lay down. It was the first time in hours that my voice didn't shake. "I will be there to perform."

CR&D

Tamara is alone, sitting next to a metal table that says Corona. She drinks tequila and has lost count of how many she's had. The waiter clears the glasses quickly. She thinks that perhaps he doesn't want to embarrass her. Or, on the contrary, he wants her to drink more so that her tip will be more generous. *One never knows with waiters.*

When she feels she is going to break into tears, she switches seats so that she is facing the wall. She stares at the poster before her: some bullfight of little importance. None of the names seem familiar. *I am one of those bulls,* she thinks, *that at first comes out fierce, and then, from all the stabbing and damn piercing, cannot go on.* She doesn't know how she is going to tell Damiana and Eduardo about Rodrigo. That she wants to be with him again. To try it, at least. She doesn't know what will happen to her father. *It's not true that you can hear us. If you could, you would have reacted when I spoke to you about the photo and put it in front of you.* She misses him. She misses his company. It is true that he wasn't always pleasant, but even that is better than his absence. It goes without saying.

She is the only one who knows the truth, and the secret of it weighs heavy on her. He told her after Damiana had gone away. When Eduardo was also gone. When her father realized that all he had left was her.

"Your sister thinks that I had your mother killed. Did you know that?"

Tamara was surprised. "How absurd. Where did she come up with such nonsense?"

Her father sat down next to her and sighed. "Tamara, someone has to know what really happened. Some day, you can tell Eduardo if you think him prudent or if he asks you, but never tell Damiana. Promise me that she'll never know. Eduardo and you are stronger."

Tamara frowned. "Well, what happened? You are starting to scare me."

Her father rubbed his face with both hands and after a long silence he looked her in the eye. "They found your mother dead with a bullet wound to the head," and to stop Tamara's reaction he gestured her to be patient; he stopped her from willful blindness. "Officially it was said that it was a mugging, that she was killed for her watch. Do you understand? But that was not the truth."

Tamara was speechless for a few seconds, not knowing how to react. "Why have you waited so long to tell me this? What happened?"

Eusebio Guerra rubbed his face over and over, as if looking for the words with his hands. He seemed almost regretful that he'd started the conversation.

"First of all, I want you to know that I didn't tell you the truth because I didn't want you to grow up distressed. In fact, I was never going to tell you what really happened, but I don't ever want you to believe what your sister does. I need you to promise me. I need to know that at least you have faith in me."

Tamara nodded.

"Your mother went out alone that day, without the driver. That seemed strange to me, it worried me. I thought she had left us, that she had left with someone who . . ." He hesitated. "That doesn't matter now. I looked through her things to see if something was missing, and at first I didn't notice anything. It was too late when I found out."

He stumbled, took a deep breath to go on, he looked away. "The gun that we kept in the cupboard was gone. I understood everything then. I went to look for her every-where. I swear to you, Tamara, we searched for her every-where. I desperately wanted to find her before . . ."

Tamara blinked, unbelieving, and looked around the room. She could have sworn that the world was falling apart before her eyes. "Before what?"

His father hugged her and Tamara broke into tears. It took her a few moments to understand what Eusebio was trying to tell her.

"We said it was a mugging. It had to be handled this way because that gave us an official justification for leav-ing, and also because I thought that it would be easier for all of you to accept. Your mother loved all three of you so much. I didn't want you to grow up thinking the opposite was true. I didn't want you to grow up feeling that you hadn't mattered to her, to think that was why she made the decision to . . . ." The words became fractured. "But Damiana left convinced that I had something to do with her death, and that's not true. Do you understand?"

Eusebio paused briefly to regain control of himself. "If Damiana finds out the real truth, she will fall apart. Your sister adored your mother. That is why I don't want you to tell her. But I want you to know. I need you to know so that you never doubt my love, and so you will forgive me."

Tamara orders another tequila and reaches for some napkins to dry her tears. She needs to muster strength from somewhere if she is going to maintain her father's wish, and not to tell Damiana the truth – if indeed it is the truth. She wishes she had the notebook on hand to write in it. She asks for a pen and writes on a dry napkin: *Don't die, please; don't die.*

Suddenly, someone grabs her from behind and she shouts with fright. It's Eduardo.

"How did you find me? Has something happened to Dad?"

"No, but we are very worried about you. We thought you had gone home and then Rodrigo told us that you hadn't stopped by there. He has been looking for you."

"Rodrigo?"

Eduardo nods with a disapproving look. Tamara observes him and remembers the night he hit her. She imagines that he is also remembering that.

"Let's go," he says at last.

"I don't want to. You go. After all, you now know where I am."

He hesitates, then sits beside her. After a deep breath he insists.

"What are you going to do if I don't go with you? Hit me or drag me out by force?"

"No. I am going to have a drink while I wait for you."

They drink in silence, and Tamara wonders if she should tell Eduardo about their father. She thinks about the rediscovered photo. Eduardo now has a very deep crease line between his eyebrows; his eyes have hardened. As she looks at him, she comes to the conclusion that if she didn't know it was the same person, she would swear that the little boy dressed like the policeman in the picture was not this man before her.

Suddenly someone begins to sing *Alma Llanera*. The song isn't halfway through before Eduardo pays the bill and he and Tamara leave in a hurry, quietly and without looking at each other. He puts his arm around her, and she rests her head on his shoulder. It is clear that those Venezuelan melodies are painful to them both.

❧ 8 ❧

I couldn't sleep. I was tossing in bed thinking of Tamara and Rodrigo, of Father in his hospital bed, of Mother's pointless death. What day was it today? I have never been able to remember dates. Somehow, I erase such details from my mental calendar.

The hotel curtains were dark and heavy, but morning pierced their edges, admonishing me that this was no time for lying down even if I had stayed up all night. So I turned on the television to ease me into the day, flipping through all the channels until I encountered one that ran episodes from old soap operas. Perhaps I would see Tamara playing some small role. The Eighties hairstyles – bangs fluffed up like meringue – were amusing, and within a few minutes the inane dialogue and ludicrously complicated plot sent me into a dark and deep slumber.

The telephone woke me. It was Tamara. Urgent. She was asking me to meet her at the hospital. The hotel's digital display clock said 10:00 – 10:00 p.m. I had slept all day.

I threw on some clothes and raced, in a cab, to the hospital. Tamara, Eduardo and Samantha (hand-in-hand like Siamese twins), stood in the waiting room in anticipation of my arrival. By the sombre looks on their faces, I knew what had happened. For some reason that I still don't understand, no tears came. *What a strange day*, I thought, and recalled a beloved teacher who had said this the day he found out about his own father's death. He was right. Days like this are strange. On the inside everything changes, and yet on the outside everything seems the same. My daily life would not change drastically with my father's absence; however, being conscious that I would never again be with him made me feel that, from now on, everything would be very different – although it was impossible to say in what way. Strange: Father's death – so feared just a few hours ago – gave me a feeling of peace that I had not felt in a very long time. Eduardo and Samantha stood silently.

Tamara mistook my reaction. "You never loved him. You don't know anything. You are an imbecile and an ingrate," she spat out the words and turned her back to me.

I was startled. I didn't want to start another argument with Tamara. Deep inside, I was glad that she was reacting with anger. Of course I loved Father. All I had really wanted was to sing for him at my next performance. *Now I am sure that you are going to hear me, Father*.

My siblings made all the arrangements for the wake and burial without me.

I went, for a short while, to the funeral home. Dimitri accompanied me. There were many people there who had not seen Tamara, Eduardo, and me since we were children. I loathed their inane comments: "You have grown so much," and "Congratulations on your success," punctuated by "I am so sorry," or "My most heartfelt condolences." There were also civil servants from other embassies, and members of the diplomatic corps we hadn't previously met. Paradoxically, I felt them to be the most sincere. They were simply doing their duty.

I stayed away from the flowers and from the little clusters of people with faces that said things like *Here I am, see me, I knew Eusebio Guerra,* and *How nice it is to see you, though it's too bad it has to be like this.* I was too young to have noticed these things when Mother died, but the fact that father's funeral had become a society event reminded me how much I hated the environment in which I had been raised.

Elena came as well, and loyally stayed at my side. I will always be thankful to her for remaining silent the entire time. She was the most prudent of all. The look in her eyes, and the hug that she gave me was enough. Thanks to her, no one else from the cast or crew came. She had let it be known that I didn't want more public fuss: I would see them at the theatre.

I couldn't believe that it was Father lying in that open silver casket. I didn't dare look. That man who I had seen shrunken in the hospital bed, who I had covered up with such care, wasn't – *is not* – Father. My father is the man who gave me that yellow duck he won in *buena lid*. The one who built Sugus towers. The one who I knew could still now hear the requiem that, by way of prayer, I softly sang for him. I'd chosen the stanza I found most fitting:

> *Supplicanti parce, Deus.*
> *Qui Mariam absolvisti,*
> *Et Ladronem exaudisti,*
> *Mhi quioque spem dedisti.*

> Forgive this supplicant, God.
> You, who absolved Mary,
> And granted the thief's prayer,
> You have given me hope, too.

A reporter asked me if I would sing the second performance of *Figaro* on Saturday at Bellas Artes. I answered, "Yes, of course," and then refused any more questions. When I left the reception, I became even more determined in my decision to adopt Michaela's technique of saving the voice for an entire day before a performance.

At Mother's burial, Father had cupped his hands around my head – his fingers weaving a helmet in attempt to protect me from the sounds. How I wished someone would have done this for me at his. But I had to be strong, make him proud. I buried all my fears, doubts, and mistrust when we buried him the next morning. And thus began my vow of silence before the performance. It would be my protection and my mourning at one and the same time.

०४९०

Tamara is at home, sitting next to the living room's window. *Dad just died last night, and once again it's not cloudy.* The sun was also shining the day her mother was buried, and Tamara feels it's unfair that there should be no clouds or rain to accompany her sadness. She has cried so much that she no longer recognizes herself in the mirror. Her eyes sting and burn. The sensation of emptiness is everywhere. It not only occupies the inside of her body, it stretches out in all directions. Pain covers each piece of furniture and each object; like a spiderweb, it obstructs her way and her vision. *What good did it do me to be your confidant, Dad? Nothing. And neither was I the smartest. You see? You were mistaken.* Tamara's body melts into the living room sofa, turning into an amorphous mass of flesh that sobs heavily under a messy head of hair. She remembers walking along on her father's arm at the embassy parties. The phone rings and someone answers. She doesn't know which of the servants it is; she cannot recognize voices – except her mother's, which is recorded with clarity in her mind. She clings to that sound. She also remembers the sounds of her Mother's flute, the accent of her Mother's words. *I forgive you, Mom. Please forgive me, too.*

After Tamara has gone through a whole box of Kleenex, the doorbell rings and Rodrigo comes in to keep her company. Tamara parts the curtains of hair hiding her face and feels how Rodrigo's arms return form and reason to her body. *Dad, your absence is water, but I shall not drown.*

❧ 9 ❧

I made myself strong in front of everyone as I moved toward the stage, and peeked through the velvet curtain to see the empty hall. The three immense storeys of red velvet seating gaped, ready to devour me: everything was in order. Nerves always stir thus. I clenched my fists and did not allow myself to falter. I was not going to break because this performance would be for Father. For Mother. And for Tamara and Eduardo, who, dressed in black, would be sitting in the audience. Samantha, the lanky panther, was with them. Rodrigo waved at me in the distance, and I corresponded.

The moment I arrived at the theatre, I unpacked the very last of the little jars from my case and arranged them according to their size and content. When Dimitri saw them, he said they looked like some kind of travelling Victorian pharmacy, and that made me laugh. I also arranged my costumes in the correct order, and turned on the humidifier before settling in to drink some tea in Dimitri's company. I enjoyed each sip, and looked at his face with care. Those ample eyebrows, now exaggerated by makeup, gave him an enigmatic air, almost wizard-like.

Then, he left me on my own. Vocalizing. Perfecting passages while I arranged my skirt. I drank more water. My throat was feeling good, ready. Only the moist palms of my hands gave away the uneasiness that was still present.

"Attention, ladies and gentlemen. First call."

In the background, the sound of the musicians tuning up could already be heard. I stopped vocalizing for a moment, and decided to quickly dust off the lightbulbs on my mirror once and for all.

"Members of the orchestra, please proceed to the pit."

The announcement caught my attention. In other opera houses, they say, "Good evening to all of you, there is half an hour left before the performance." And then: "There are fifteen minutes." And finally: "There are five minutes left. Everyone please take your places." At the end, each soloist is called individually by name. The other evening I hadn't noticed that it was done differently here. Perhaps it was worth mentioning it to Marilú afterwards.

I had heard that Marisita, the choir director, was telling anyone who would listen that I shouldn't have been allowed to sing, that they should have used an understudy. (Those sopranos who have done little with their own careers can be very persistent about those of others.) And such was her influence that the director of the Institute of Fine Arts (how was it possible I still didn't remember his name? Mr. Who?) had come to the funeral home and repeated his offer to find me a replacement. He sent the message through Eduardo because I had already left. I imagine that the director brought someone in to take my place in case I failed – likely someone from the San Francisco or Los Angeles opera companies, as they have the most accessible supply – but he had been kind enough not to let me know. Perhaps Juan José and Guido had a hand in making sure I was left alone. Their support and vows of trust kept me from collapsing under the bureaucratic pressures. I could not let them down.

The second call did not take me by surprise. As I vocalized, each note grew exact, and vibrated with harmony, and the rat that I usually felt churning in my stomach was hardly moving. Outside, I could hear the laughter of my fellow performers as they moved from one dressing room to another with an enthusiasm that I didn't want to participate in, but that I shared from a distance. People's steps coming and going. An unstoppable parade behind the bevelled glass of my door. Juan José, Guido, Michaela, Elena, and Faustina, had all come to see me at some point. I suppose they secretly wanted to make sure I was ready to go onstage, but they showed only affection and encouragement. It seems that the little bald guy from the *Informador* had liked the first performance, after all – he was there again that night. He had written a good review that I didn't wish to see. I would read it on the plane on my way to some other engagement. The technician who spoke perfect Italian peeked into my dressing room and told me not to worry – that he would tell Maestra Marisita to go "fam culo."

Just when I thought that everyone possible had dropped by and that I would be left in peace for the last minutes, Tamara and Eduardo arrived.

"You forgot this," Eduardo said, giving me the notebook. "I don't know if you still need it. In truth, I took the liberty of adding a few things."

I smiled. Even though I had been vaguely thinking about Marilú, I had completely forgotten about the notebook, that I had to return it to her. It was then that Tamara said to me, "The one who set the bad example was me. I wrote in it the other day when I was waiting for you."

A brief leaf through its pages made me realize that I could never return the journal to Marilú. I felt enormous curiosity when I saw my siblings' handwriting. Perhaps, without trying, we had found a new way to communicate with each other.

"No one is going to read this except us. I will keep it."

Tamara and Eduardo hugged me and left in silence. They had to hurry to get to their seats on time. I hadn't said it to Tamara and Eduardo, but I was thankful that Samantha had remained outside, that she had granted the three of us those few moments alone – even if I was getting used to her eternal shadow.

I drank a sip of water and walked toward the window. My fake eyelashes were perfectly in place, and the purple dress was snug at my waist. The voices of my fellow singers doing scales and rehearsing different passages mingled – through the speakers and the thin dressing room walls – with my own. Through the window, I could see that Eje Central Avenue was jammed with traffic and frantic drivers. I had asked to have the horrible and useless curtain removed, and I could now see the Palacio de Correos in all its beauty as the sun was setting. The cacophony of the musicians tuning up fell like a dirty waterfall from the speaker in the ceiling. *Yes, the damn speaker again.* I clenched my teeth and after a long pause, I was ready to leave my dressing room.

Without a doubt, the blow, the late arriving whiplash that sadness always brings, would come – but not that night. My family smiled at me from the photograph posted on the mirror. I turned the knob and opened the door. Dimitri was waiting for me so we could enter the wings together. The overture began. Elena approached and excitedly told me that no one had brought televisions that night, and that even the timpanist had returned from Acapulco, and was in position. Someone whispered *"in bocca al luppo,"* and almost in unison we replied, *"Creppi il luppo."* The overture began with a contagious vitality and energy. We stopped our whispering and stood in silence, surrendering ourselves to the rhythm and humour of each beat. At last, Dimitri took my hand, and I let myself be taken toward the embrace of the bright lights.

Acknowledgements

The first draft of this manuscript was written in Spanish, during the three-day-frenzy of the Muskoka Novel Marathon in Huntsville, the summer I arrived to live in Toronto. I have stopped counting the number of drafts there have been since that first attempt to tell this story – the time and effort put into the making of this book have been enormous. Even so, I wish to thank the organizers of this absolutely crazy and memorable yearly event, which provides a much needed venue for writers like me – who have impossibly busy lives – to escape reality and dive into nonstop writing. I can't wait to go back!

I want to thank my beloved husband, Edgar, who has always supported my passion for writing. Cielo: I'm so lucky to have you. I also need to thank my three children, Ivana, Natalia, and Marco, who have grown up having to share mom with her writing. You make my life happy every day.

The Wolf's Mouth/Damiana's Reprieve has had three different printings in Spanish, and was recently published in French. The first Spanish edition came out in Santo Domingo, Dominican Republic, with the prestigious Casa de Teatro.

The second printing of this book was done in the State of Mexico, by the now-defunct Instituto Mexiquense de Cultura. That edition was soon out of print, so Editorial Ink in Mexico City took over and published it as an e-book, which became *Boca de lobo*'s third Spanish edition and is the only one still available at this point.

In the spring of 2018 *Boca de lobo* appeared as *La Gueule du Loup*, in a beautiful translation by Khristina Legault, published by Lugar Común Editorial in Ottawa, as the first title of their new In Medias Res series. So, to cut it short, this little book has been the gift that keeps on giving, and I couldn't be more grateful or more proud.

The Canadian edition of *Damiana's Reprieve* is a dream come true for me. I want to state my gratitude to Barry and Michael Callaghan for opening the doors of Exile Editions to my writing. I feel very honoured.

Barry and Michael: Thank you for your patience and encouragement as we went through the necessary revisions of the manuscript. You made me feel safe and protected; I will always be thankful for your generosity. Thanks to Gabriela Campos as well, for being such a great friend and supporter of my work. And very special thanks to Gustavo Escobedo for translating *Boca de lobo* into *The Wolf's Mouth/Damiana's Reprieve*, Jerry Tutunjian and Lisa Foad for revising and editing the English manuscript, and to Nina Callaghan not only for kindly helping with the final revisions, but for welcoming me in her home to work on the manuscript until it was complete. I learned a lot through this process and am deeply thankful for the generous support you all gave me.

I must also thank some special friends, whose generous feedback improved many aspects of this story. A big GRACIAS goes out to my favourite singer – whom I am very fortunate to call my friend – Rolando Villazón, and his beautiful and courageous wife Lucy, whose input was instrumental in bettering my understanding of the operatic world; Mexican music critic Lázaro Azar, and Luis Gutiérrez Ruvalcaba, Kurt Herman and Manuel Yrízar, all of whom helped me build the characters' musical backgrounds; Dr. Enrique Berebichez in Mexico City, who contributed to the medical aspects of this story; Adriana Jiménez de Sada, who polished the very first version of the Spanish manuscript and pointed me in the right direction; the late Mexican writer Daniel Sada, who always encouraged me to keep on writing, and whom I am very honoured to have called my mentor and friend.

My Fairy Godmother, Dr. Gillian Bartlett: I have learned so much from you! Thank you for your time, patience and generosity. Thank you for your guidance in order to finish the last round of corrections of this book.

And last, but not least, a most heartfelt thank you to all my friends both near and far. Each one of you knows how special and unique you are to me, and how grateful I feel for the bond – and the stories – we have shared thus far.

Publisher's note

In 2009 Exile Editions released this book under the title *The Wolf's Mouth* but, due to an unfortunate oversight during a change in distributors at that time, that original edition did not make it into stores as expected. And so we now have this new edition, with a new title (so as to not confuse the two versions) making its way to stores across North America.